WRONG WEDDING

CONVENIENT MARRIAGES

NOELLE ADAMS

1

On the afternoon of her best friend's father's funeral, Summer Cray wished she was feeling better.

She was exhausted from a particularly busy time at work and from weeks of supporting Carter as he dealt with his father's diagnosis of pancreatic cancer, which had led up to his death two months later. She had a headache, and putting on a polite, sympathetic face for the funeral of a man she'd intensely disliked was the last thing she wanted to be doing. But Carter Wilson had been her best friend since they'd been in preschool. He'd sat next to her at their craft table and told her that her finger painting was the best in the class, which had meant the world to an orphaned girl as painfully shy as she'd been.

Carter's relationship with his father was conflicted, but that didn't mean he wasn't grieving the loss. A conflicted relationship didn't mean grief was lessened. Sometimes it just made it even harder.

So despite the pounding of her head—from either tension or dehydration or both—Summer kept a composed expression and exerted the effort to make comforting small talk with the Wilsons' large extended family who had come in for the funeral. Carter was pale, and he was having trouble talking—like he was still recovering from a blow—so she rarely left his side.

The family was mingling in the large reception rooms of the Wilson mansion in Green Valley, North Carolina. A variety of snacks were being served, but most of the thirty or so people present were more interested in the drinks than the food. The memorial service was scheduled for one o'clock, followed by the graveside service.

It was going to be a long day, and it had barely started.

Carter was only a few months older than Summer. He'd just turned thirty-two. He was tall and fit and had movie-star good looks. It was impossible to look at him and not feel instinctive pleasure at the way his face and body were put together. There were shadows under his brown eyes today, however, and his high cheekbones seemed to be cut sharper than usual. They'd just been chatting with a distant cousin who lived in California, but as the man wandered away, Summer turned to Carter.

"You doing okay?"

He tugged at his hair in a restless gesture that wasn't at all like him. "Yeah. I'm fine."

"Do you need a break? You don't need to be *on* the whole time, you know."

"But I do. Otherwise Mom will have to do everything, and she's had a hard enough time as it is."

As far as Summer could see, Mrs. Wilson was doing better than Carter was. The woman was a master socializer, and she was clearly in her element right now—basking in even more attention than she normally received. She'd always been one of the queens of Green Valley, a small town outside Charlotte with a disproportionately high percentage of wealthy people because it had been developed forty years ago around an exclusive country club and marina on the large boating lake. Even as the Wilson fortune dwindled with the decline of the family hotel business, Mrs. Wilson's central position in the town social life never wavered.

But Summer wasn't about to argue with Carter at a time like this. "Okay. I'm going to run to the bathroom real quick. I'll be back soon."

"Sure." He smiled at her. The sweet, Carter-like smile she'd known and loved all her life. Then he leaned over and brushed a kiss on her cheek.

She blinked at the unexpected gesture. "What was that for?"

"For everything."

She gave him a trembling smile before she left the room. When she'd reached the nearest bathroom and saw it was occupied, she kept going, heading toward another bathroom farther down the hall. She peed and washed her hands and stared at herself in the mirror for a minute.

She looked just as pale and haggard as Carter did. She had ash-blond hair and big brown eyes and clear skin that was naturally rosy. She had a fit, curvy body and an appearance often described as *wholesome*—like she should have been a Midwestern farm girl instead of the only heir to a fortune made a hundred years ago when her great-grandfather established a global candy empire with a brand that remained a household name.

Summer wasn't any sort of beauty queen, but she was

used to seeing a pleasant reflection in the mirror. She smiled automatically to smooth out her face, tucking back a few strands of hair that had escaped from her low bun. She found a couple of stray ibuprofens in her purse and swallowed them, hoping they would lessen the headache.

She wanted to go home. Go to bed. Turn out the lights and pull the blankets up over her head. She was in no mood to celebrate the life of a man who'd been nothing but greedy and selfish and manipulative and heartless to his family, bullying his free-spirited wife into compliance and taking advantage of both his sons.

But she couldn't. Carter needed her. He'd always been like family to her when she had no one else. Her parents had died when she was an infant when their private plane had crashed, and she'd been raised by a well-intentioned but distant grandmother who'd always been convinced Summer wasn't strong enough to handle the fortune she'd inherit. For many, many years, Carter had been the most important person in her life. The only one who knew, loved, and trusted her for real. So she squared her shoulders, took a few deep breaths, and left the bathroom.

She was passing the library a few doors down when motion in the room caught her attention, so she paused to look in.

Her heart gave a weird little jump when she saw the person in the room was Lincoln Wilson, Carter's older brother.

Lincoln was three years older than her and Carter, so she'd never spent much time with him. She'd known him mostly from Carter's complaints about him and from a lot of sarcastic, mocking comments he'd aimed at her whenever she was in his presence. He'd had a huge blowup with his family when he was in college—unsurprising given the way Arthur Wilson had treated them—and after that, Lincoln had broken ties completely. He didn't work for Wilson Hotels the way Carter did. He didn't attend family functions or make an effort to stay close to his younger brother. And he didn't even have the good sense to move away and start up life in a new city where he could have been anonymous.

Instead, he was a bartender at one of the two high-end bars in Green Valley, serving expensive drinks and making smart-ass comments to his former friends and classmates. Summer saw him there occasionally and tried very hard to ignore the obnoxious smirk he always aimed at her.

At the moment, Lincoln was standing by himself in front of an oil portrait of his father. His back was to the door. His black T-shirt was made of a thick, soft material and lay perfectly against his broad shoulders and straight back, and his dark trousers were well tailored, but the outfit was completely inappropriate for the occasion. Every other man present was wearing a suit.

She hadn't had a conversation longer than two minutes with Lincoln for years. He knew her favorite drinks at his bar and would often predict her order before she made it. He'd occasionally say something taunting about whichever man happened to be her date, and he'd comment laughingly whenever she had on a new outfit or did something different with her hair. Last year, she'd been on a first date with a real asshole. Lincoln must have overheard, and he'd come around the bar, grabbed the man by the back of his shirt, and propelled him out of the building without a single word, leaving Summer torn between relief that she hadn't had to end the date herself (since she hated confrontation) and annoyance at Lincoln's presumptuous intrusion in her business.

Since they weren't friends or even polite acquaintances, she was about to duck out of the library unseen when he said without turning around, "Are you going to say hi to your best friend's big brother, or are you just going to stand there, fluttering like a nervous butterfly?"

She gulped. He hadn't even turned his head. She had no idea how he'd known she was there.

"You didn't look like you wanted a greeting." Her voice was much cooler than she used with anyone else. He'd been infuriating her since she was eight years old, and he'd given her a long, unwanted lecture on how she was kicking a soccer ball wrong. "And I wasn't doing anything remotely resembling *fluttering*."

He turned his head in her direction with a flash of a smile. His typical dry, arrogant smile. Not a real one. "I could feel your fluttering from all the way across the room."

Summer was a friendly, even-tempered person. Most people liked her. No one got into arguments or fights with her. She was quiet and tended toward shyness, but she genuinely cared about other people, and she liked for other people to like her back. The only bad feeling she ever provoked in others was the occasional resentment or envy of the family fortune she'd inherited, which was a completely understandable reaction as far as she was concerned. She didn't deserve to be given so much money—not when everyone else had to work for everything they got. She'd spent her life trying to make up for what felt like an injustice by being intentionally generous and empathetic.

She almost never felt so angry she wanted to snap her teeth at someone else, but she did right now. And she didn't have the mental energy to control it the way she normally would. "Maybe what you've inaccurately identified as *fluttering* is normal human feelings of sympathy and concern. How would you know since human feeling is utterly foreign to you?"

"So you're saying you were lurking in the doorway of the room because you felt sorry for me?" Lincoln had the same handsome features as Carter, but his hair was a darker brown, his eyebrows thicker, and his eyes a startling shade of green. While Carter's handsomeness came across as safe and solid and steady, Lincoln's came across as dangerous.

Sexy, but dangerous.

Summer didn't want to see either one in this man, and the fact that she did—that her skin had flushed and her heartbeat had accelerated with an involuntary surge of the attraction she always felt around him—made her angrier than ever. She stepped farther into the room, closer to him. "No, I don't feel sorry for you. The sympathy and concern I'm feeling are not aimed at you."

He'd turned all the way around now, and he gave a soft huff of ironic amusement. "Oh, I know. They're all reserved for my brother. Poor put-upon saint that he is."

"You have no reason to talk about him that way. He's never done anything to you. If you're mad at your father, then fine. He definitely deserved it. But Carter doesn't. He's having a hard time, and a brother with any sort of heart would try to be there for him instead of skulking in corners and making rude comments to people who are trying to help."

Lincoln moved closer to her. Way too close. Only a few

inches away. He had a habit of invading personal space that way. Summer knew it was an intimidation tactic, and she had to fight not to shy back from him and let him score a victory.

He murmured, "Whatever gave you the impression that I have a heart?"

"Nothing. Nothing gave me that impression. Anyone who's looking for a heart in you is going to be woefully disappointed."

"We clearly understand each other." He smiled again, the corner of his lips turning up. Way too sexily. She could see dark bristles on his jaw and down his neck. She could see the thick fringe of dark lashes contrasting with the vivid color of his eyes.

Her heart was pounding. Throbbing. In her chest. In her ears. In her headache.

"We don't understand each other at all. I'll never understand someone who can treat his family the way you treat Carter. He's tried to reach out to you over and over again, and you give him nothing but a cold shoulder."

"Well, you treat him well enough for both of us, so I feel sure he's in good hands." There was a bitter edge to his tone, but it was light. Casually dismissive. As if she were nothing.

Summer couldn't remember ever hating another person —not even Carter's father—as much as she hated Lincoln right now. She was shaking with it. She couldn't form a single word through the tightness of her throat.

Lincoln arched his thick eyebrows. "Nothing? I was hoping for a cold, self-righteous comeback. Only appropriate for a villain like me."

Her hands tightened at her sides. Her mind was an angry whirl of feeling, but she couldn't think of a single thing to say to express it. She had friends who could always come up with the perfect, clever thing to say—no matter the state of their emotions—but she'd never been like that.

When she was in her normal, composed state of mind, she could converse like an intelligent, articulate human being. But when she was upset, her mind went infuriatingly blank.

Lincoln let out a soft huff of dry amusement. "All right then. Maybe you'll have more to say about your upcoming nuptials. I hear congratulations are in order."

She was so surprised her whole body jerked. Like she'd suddenly run into a brick wall. "Carter told you?"

"He did. Some remnant of brotherly feeling, I guess."

"Or maybe he wanted to make sure you didn't do anything to sabotage it."

"Could be." He was giving her that mocking smile, and she wanted to scratch it right off his face. "Or maybe he knew I'd try to talk him out of the lunatic plan."

"It's not a lunatic plan. It's a practical strategy for dealing with a problem. It changes nothing."

"Are you serious? You'll be married to Carter. He isn't in love with you, but you're going to let him marry you anyway so you can hand him your inheritance and let him toss it into the black hole that's Wilson Hotels." He was still standing too close to her. Way too close. Despite his cool, arrogant manner, he was shuddering with reined-in energy. She didn't know what it was, but she could see it in him now.

It was making her shudder too. She rubbed her aching head and snapped, "I'm not handing him my inheritance. I'm investing a very small portion of it in a company Carter has spent years working to grow. We'll be married for a few months until the acquisition goes through. It's all set up and in the works. Once it's done, we'll get divorced. It changes nothing."

For almost a century, Wilson Hotels had been known for their old-fashioned luxury and personalized service. Unfortunately, that kind of luxury came with a very high price tag, and the company hadn't earned a profit for decades. In the past twenty years, they'd had to close more than half their properties. Carter had been pouring himself into saving the company and had made a deal with a regional midpriced hotel chain to acquire their properties and fold them into the Wilson brand, branching out into a price range that had a better chance of success in today's world. It was a good plan. A wise acquisition. But his father had outright rejected it. So after Carter had learned of his father's diagnosis, he'd come up with one last-ditch strategy for saving the Wilson family company.

Summer had a huge inheritance and was more than willing to invest in Carter's plans for the business, but she was hampered by an unreasonable trust fund that severely limited the ways in which she could use her fortune until she was thirty-five years old. But she'd found one loophole in the fine print of the trust.

All she had to do was marry Carter. Then when he got control of the company after his father's death, she'd be able to invest in it and Carter would be able to salvage his family's legacy.

She loved and believed in Carter. She didn't care if marrying as a business arrangement was a weird thing to do. The truth was, in a town as wealthy and insular as Green

Valley, marriages had been made and broken for far stranger reasons.

Lincoln evidently thought differently. He shook his head slowly. "Both of you are out of your minds. I can kind of understand Carter. He's desperate and still trying to prove something to our dad even though the bastard is dead and soon to be buried. He doesn't know you're in love with him. But *you*... you know better than this."

She gasped and took a clumsy step backward. She didn't care if it proved he'd scored a point. She had to get some distance. "I'm not in love with Carter!"

"Of course you are. At least you think you are. He's been the prince in all your daydreams since you were a kid."

"We're friends! We've always just been friends."

"I know that. But that doesn't stop you from wanting more." His expression was its normal indifference, but his voice had a bitter edge that she didn't understand. "Are you really going to stand there and tell me you don't? That you're not indulging in ridiculous fantasies about this practical marriage finally opening his eyes and showing him that his fated soul mate has been right beside him all the time? I've seen the movies and heard all the sappy songs too. And I'm telling you right now that it's never going to happen. Carter loves you, but he's never going to love you like *that*."

"You... you... you... *dick*!" She wished she could come up with a more crushing insult, but that was the only word that came to her. She couldn't remember ever being so angry in her life. So torn open and exposed. The fury and humiliation crashed into her, blurring her eyes, spinning her aching head. "You have... no idea who I am or what I want. How dare you stand there and act like you know me."

"Of course I know you. I've known you for most of our lives. And can I remind you of your prom? When you went with Carter as a friend while secretly hoping for it to turn into more. Then you spent most of the evening crying in the bathroom because he danced the whole time with someone else."

"How... how did you...?" She was swaying on her feet now. Her head hurt so much it was making her stomach churn. There was a real possibility she was going to pass out.

"How did I know it? Everyone knew it. You really think you were hiding your crush from the world?" His voice snapped like a whip. If she were thinking clearer, she might wonder why he seemed so angry about a topic that didn't directly affect him, but it was all she could do to stay on her feet. "Carter isn't the one who needs to open his eyes. *You* do. And if you marry him for such a ridiculous reason, you're going to live to regret it. You're better than this, Summer."

"*Better*?" She choked on the word. "What the fuck do you know about being better? You who've done nothing with your life but throw it away to spite your father."

"At least I haven't wasted it on daydreams about a man who is never going to want me."

Summer slapped him.

She actually *slapped* him.

She wasn't a violent person. She wasn't an angry person. Everyone always called her nice. Sweet. A natural peacemaker. The last time she'd hit someone had been in kindergarten when a classmate had stolen her chocolate cupcake.

She was so stunned by the slap that she froze, her hand poised in midair. It was trembling. Her whole body was trembling. Her palm stung from the impact with his cheek.

Lincoln was evidently caught by surprise too. He stared at her, one of his cheeks slightly reddened from the slap. His lips were parted just slightly.

"You don't get to talk to me like that," she finally managed to rasp. There were tears in her eyes, but she wasn't about to let them fall. "You don't get to talk to me at all."

She had to escape before she completely fell apart, so she turned on her heel and hurried out of the room.

She made it to the bathroom before she threw up.

WHEN SHE'D EMPTIED her stomach, she cried on the floor of the bathroom for a few minutes. Then she stayed there in a heap, too physically and emotionally exhausted to even move.

The worst thing about the whole situation was that Lincoln might have been right about her.

She *had* been daydreaming about Carter since she was a girl. She'd been his friend. Completely and truly his friend. But on any given moment in the past fifteen years, she would have leaped into his arms had he given her even the slightest indication he was interested in a romantic relationship.

She hadn't wasted her life on the crush, no matter what Lincoln had said. She dated regularly, and she'd had serious relationships with three different men. None of them had lasted more than a year, but that wasn't because of Carter. It was because they just hadn't felt right. It had felt like she'd been playing a role with them rather than being herself. She'd done well in college and then earned a master's in nonprofit administration. For the past six years, she'd had a job fund-raising for Hope House, a local nonprofit that ran a food bank, a youth center, and a literacy program for people in need.

She loved her job, and she believed in the work she was doing.

After being a lonely child, she now had a circle of true friends.

She hadn't thrown her life away on futile daydreams, but the hope of something developing with Carter had lingered like a whisper at the back of her mind.

Maybe it was something she needed to deal with.

Maybe it was time to put it aside for good.

But Lincoln was the last person in the world who had a right to tell her that.

She wasn't sure how long she would have stayed sprawled out on the floor of the bathroom, but eventually there was a knock on the door.

"Summer?" It was Carter's voice. He sounded concerned. "Are you okay?"

"Y-yeah. I'm fine." Her throat ached from vomiting. She tried to straighten up.

"Lincoln said you might be sick. Can I come in?"

It took effort, but she managed to regain her feet. She unlocked the door and slowly opened it.

Carter's eyes were worried, and his mouth twisted as he took in her appearance. "Shit, Summer. You *are* sick."

"I'm not sick. Not really. I just have a headache." She glanced in the mirror and saw what he saw. Her skin was damp and pale. Half her hair had slipped out of the bun. There were dark shadows under her eyes.

She looked terrible.

"Did you throw up? Lincoln said you were sick."

She swallowed hard over the pain in her throat. She felt trembly and weak, and she didn't like feeling that way. "How did he...?" She'd been in the bathroom with the door closed before she threw up. She had absolutely no idea how Lincoln could have known about it. Had he followed her and heard through the door?

"I don't know. But he was worried about you and came to get me. I'm not sure what got into him since he normally doesn't give a crap about other people, but I'm glad he did." Carter came into the bathroom, took a washcloth, and got it wet in the sink. Then he gently wiped her clammy skin with it. "You should go on home."

Even the day before, she'd have been touched and breathless at the tender way he was wiping her face, but for some reason it made her feel weird now. She moved away from his touch and smiled at him. "I'm not going home, Carter. I don't feel great, but I'm not sick. It's really just a headache that got out of control. I'm not going to miss your dad's funeral. I'm not."

Carter scanned her face and evidently satisfied himself with the state of her health. "Okay. Thank you. Can I get you anything?"

"Well, I threw up my Advil so I could use some more. And maybe a Coke."

"Let's go get that for you then."

She felt a little better as they left the bathroom. Her head still pounded, but she wasn't so weak and dizzy. When they turned a corner of the hall, she was suddenly face-to-face with Lincoln.

He was standing by himself in the hallway, leaning

against the wall in a casual, unconcerned pose. But his expression was sober. Oddly quiet. He was holding a glass bottle of Coke in his hand.

Her eyes met his, and she couldn't look away. She didn't understand the expression there, but it made her chest ache, her breath hitch.

Without saying a word, he handed her the bottle of Coke. It was cold and slightly damp from condensation. The cap was already off.

She accepted it, staring down at it in astonishment. When she looked back up at Lincoln's face, he was watching her with that same focused intensity.

He wasn't the sort of man who ever apologized. Maybe this was as close as he got.

"Thanks," she mumbled, taking a sip of the Coke. It was good. Really good. She couldn't believe he'd gotten it for her.

He'd just been meaner to her than anyone else ever had.

Carter looked between her and his brother. Then said, "Come on. Let's go find you some Advil."

They left Lincoln standing by himself in the hall. Summer glanced over her shoulder once to see that he was watching her as she left.

FIVE HOURS LATER, Summer was back in the Wilson mansion. The funeral and graveside service were over, but the house was filled with friends and acquaintances who'd stopped by to pay their respects.

Summer still had the headache, but it had lessened to a

dull throbbing. The day was almost over. Pretty soon she could go home and go to bed.

She was still at Carter's side where she'd remained most of the day. He seemed to have relaxed a bit, and he wasn't quite so pale. He was obviously exhausted, but she thought maybe he was doing better.

At the moment, they were talking to Lance Carlyle, who'd grown up with them in Green Valley. Summer had always liked Lance, with his thick auburn curls and his clever, insouciant manner. His expression was more sober than normal today as he came up to shake Carter's hand and express his sympathy.

"It's got to be hard, it happening so fast," Lance said.

Carter nodded. "It is. But we had a couple of months to prepare, and it's probably best he didn't linger for a long time in pain."

"That's true. Do you know what's going to happen to the business?"

"He always told me he was leaving it to me. I'm the only one who wants it."

"Yeah." Lance glanced over Summer's shoulder, and she looked back to see Lincoln standing by himself, leaning against a wall, and sipping a glass of whiskey. "I guess so."

Carter looked over too and saw what Summer had seen. "Lincoln has made it clear for fifteen years that he wants nothing to do with the company. I believe him. He's not expecting anything from Dad. He probably wouldn't take Dad's money even if he was offered any of it. Which he won't be."

When Summer glanced over again, Lincoln turned his head and caught her eye. Their gazes met across the room for just a little too long, and she was breathless when she made herself turn away.

The man was way too intense. It was unnerving. She didn't like it at all.

She started to say something to Lance—just a casual comment to keep the conversation moving—when his wife, Savannah, joined them.

Savannah had been in Summer's grade all through school, but they'd never really been friends. Savannah hadn't been in Summer's social circle, and she'd always had a slight chip on her shoulder, making it hard for people to get close to her. Plus Summer had known that Carter was kind of into Savannah in high school, and Summer had been jealous.

Jealous. She didn't like that about herself, but it was true.

She felt stupid now because Savannah had become a friend over the past couple of years, ever since she'd married Lance and they started hanging out in the same circles. Summer really liked the other woman, and she wished she could be as quick and articulate as Savannah was.

Maybe she'd have an easier time holding her own with Lincoln if she had a tongue as sharp as Savannah's.

Savannah hugged Carter, and then she hugged Summer. She asked how they were doing, and the conversation turned again to Carter's emotional state and what was likely to happen to Wilson Hotels.

After a few minutes, Summer looked over her shoulder again. It was supposed to be a quick look—just to see what Lincoln was doing now and whether he still wasn't talking to anyone—but their eyes met again.

He must have some sort of creepy sixth sense that alerted him when anyone happened to look in his direction.

When she felt a twisting tension in her chest, Summer checked to confirm that Carter was fine, chatting with Lance and Savannah, and then she walked over to where Lincoln was standing.

He arched his eyebrows as she approached and straightened up from where he'd been leaning against the wall but said nothing.

When she reached him, she opened her mouth. No words came out.

His questioning look turned into a slight frown. "You okay?" His tone was mild. Not particularly concerned.

She nodded. Swallowed hard. Stared at the floor for a few seconds before she glanced up and said, "I'm sorry."

He blinked.

"For slapping you," she added since he looked so surprised.

His expression relaxed slightly. "Ah. Well. I deserved it."

"It doesn't matter if you deserved it or not. I shouldn't have done it. So I'm sorry."

His agile mouth turned up at one corner. "Apology accepted."

His expression gave her the weirdest feeling. She wasn't sure what it was, but it was akin to excitement. It was a highly disturbing response to nothing more than a half smile, so she took a step back. "Anyway. I wanted to say that. This doesn't mean I don't still despise you."

He twitched his eyebrows in an obnoxiously smug way. "I would have been deeply disappointed in you if you'd stopped."

She rolled her eyes and turned away from him to return to Carter. It felt like he was watching her as she left him, but she resisted the impulse to turn back and check.

~

THREE DAYS LATER, Summer was sitting in a waiting area of an attorney's office, fiddling with her phone and hoping everything was going well for Carter.

He, Lincoln, and his mother were in with the attorney for the reading of Arthur Wilson's will. There shouldn't be any surprises. They'd all known for years that Mrs. Wilson would get the estate, Carter would get the company, and Lincoln would get nothing.

They'd been in there for more than an hour now, however, and Summer was getting restless. Anxious. She wanted Carter to come out so she'd know for sure that their plans could go forward.

She wasn't sure why, but the conversation with Lincoln before the funeral a few days ago had killed the last lingering hope she'd been holding on to for a romantic future with Carter. The old feelings were completely gone now. Vanished into nothing. Leaving no trace except a faint embarrassment that she'd been so stupid for so long. She had no idea how it had happened, but she felt free in a way she couldn't remember feeling.

It was ironic that she had Lincoln to thank for that. Not that it excused his wretched behavior.

She was still planning to help Carter out by marrying him for a few months until his planned acquisition had gone through. There was no reason not to—now that she wasn't harboring any sort of silly fantasies about what it might lead to. He was still her best friend, and he needed her. He was usually a stable, levelheaded person, but he'd felt almost desperate to her lately, like losing his father before he'd been able to prove himself to him had pushed him over the edge.

If she could help him work through that desperation, then she was going to do it.

The practical marriage wouldn't affect anything negatively in her life. She wasn't dating anyone at the moment. She wasn't even particularly interested in dating right now. She wanted to go through with the plan and see it to the end, and then she could start fresh.

Maybe find something new to be excited about.

But none of that could happen until Carter came out of the office and told her that their plans were a go.

She waited ten more minutes before the office door opened. She jumped to her feet as Carter appeared in the doorway.

She knew immediately that something was wrong. His face was pale. His forehead was furrowed. And his eyes were stunned and pained.

"What happened?" she asked, hurrying over to meet him halfway.

He started to say something and shook his head instead.

"Carter?" Her voice was sharp from concern. "What happened?"

"The bastard didn't leave Carter the company." The voice came from behind them. It was low and bitter and familiar.

Summer turned to see Lincoln walking up to them with a snarl on his handsome face. "What? What are you talking about? He was supposed to leave it to Carter."

"I know that," Lincoln muttered. "But he was a bastard to the very end. He left it to me."

"*What*?" Summer's voice cracked with her astonishment. Her eyes shot between Carter's pained face and Lincoln's angry one. "Why would he...?"

"Because he wanted to punish me and keep controlling Carter." Lincoln was almost shaking with repressed rage. There could be no mistake at all about his response to this news. He wasn't pleased. He wasn't smug or gloating or victorious. This was the last thing in the world he'd wanted, and he was furious about it. "There's no other explanation for his doing this to us. He hated me, and this was his final twist of the knife."

"But it's Carter who's being punished. Carter never did anything but stay loyal and support him. How could he do this to Carter?"

"He was probably worried that Carter was making plans for the company that he didn't agree with, so this was his last effort at exerting control. That's all the asshole ever cared about."

"It doesn't matter," Carter rasped. "It's done. We're stuck with it. We need to just figure out where to go from here."

"That's easy," Lincoln said. "If the company is mine, then I'll give it to you. It's yours now. I don't want anything to do with it."

Summer relaxed at those words. "Oh. Good. That's good then. If Lincoln will give it to you, then we're okay. We can still go through with the marriage and the acquisition and—"

"No, we can't," Carter interrupted. "It will take time for the will to go through and then more time to implement the transfer from Lincoln to me. It's not going to be finalized in time for the acquisition. There's a timeline on the deal—basically just a month—and there's no way we'll make it. We'll have lost the chance. We might as well just declare bankruptcy and be done with it."

"Oh no." Summer put a hand on her stomach, which was twisting with anxiety. "What are we going to do then?" She wasn't sure why she looked over to Lincoln for an answer, but she did.

He was dressed just as inappropriately as ever in dark-washed jeans and a gray V-neck. He was big and sexy and dangerous and simmering with anger. "What about this? You do your stupid marriage thing and get the money for the investment. I'll sign off on the acquisition, and then we'll transfer ownership of the company."

Carter's face shifted to hope for the first time since he'd left the office, which made Summer want to cry.

"It won't work," she said. "It's the terms of my ridiculous trust. I can't take out that amount of money to invest in anything but a family business. *My* family business. Which means I need to be connected to it by marriage. That's the only loophole I've been able to find. If the company is Lincoln's, it won't work."

"Why the hell did your grandma set up the trust that way?" Lincoln looked vaguely outraged.

"Because she came from a different time. She was afraid I'd be taken advantage of by men trying to get at my money. She thought I was too nice. Not strong enough. That I'd be too easily misled. I'll have full access to the money when I turn thirty-five, but not before then."

Lincoln made a frustrated sound, but he didn't question her further.

Of course it was a ridiculous trust. It was framed in a way that treated her like a child even though she was a thirty-one-year-old woman with a career and intelligence and maturity. She'd tried for several years to find other legal loopholes around the restrictive clauses, but there was nothing she could do.

If she wanted to invest a lot of money in a company, she had to marry into it.

"I know," Carter said abruptly. "I know what we can do." He looked strained and unnaturally controlled and not at all like himself.

He looked like a desperate man and not like the Carter she'd always known.

"What?" Summer reached for his arm, wanting to support him since it felt like he might fall apart at any moment.

"You can marry Lincoln instead."

"No!" Summer responded sharply.

"No!" Lincoln said at the exact same time and with even more vehemence.

"Why not? It would work. The marriage is just going to be on paper, no matter who it is you're married to. Nothing will change. We have the prenup already made up. We'd just need to switch my name to Lincoln's. Then you'd be able to use your trust fund for the investment. The acquisition would go through. And you could get divorced exactly as planned."

"You're not thinking straight right now," Lincoln said, taking a step closer in that intense way he had. "I know how much you've put into this deal, and I know what it means to you, but you can't ask your best friend to marry a man she despises. You can't do that to her."

"It doesn't matter if she likes you or not. She doesn't have to live with you. You just need to be married on paper. Right?" He turned toward Summer with a look that was achingly anxious.

She swallowed hard, looking between Carter and Lincoln. "I... guess."

"Don't you dare do this, Summer," Lincoln muttered. "Don't you dare agree to it. There have got to be limits to the extent to which you'll sacrifice yourself on his altar."

"I'm not sacrificing myself." Her mind was still whirling. She wasn't sure why she was saying those words. She wasn't sure why it felt like she meant them. "I'm not. Carter is right. It's just on paper. What does it matter?"

Lincoln was almost choking on his outrage. "What...? How...?" He turned away abruptly with a throaty sound of absolute frustration. "I'm not going to do it. You can both be stupid all you want, but I'm not going to go along with it. You can have the company. It's yours. But I'm not going to go through with this farce of a marriage."

"Yes, you will." Carter straightened up to his full height and met his brother's eyes. They were the same size. The same breadth of their shoulders. They stared each other down. "You're going to do it."

"I will not—"

"You owe me." Carter's tone was stone cold. Summer had never heard anything like it from her friend before. "You know you do. You owe me, and this is how you're going to repay the debt."

Lincoln froze for a few seconds. Then his face twisted dramatically. "Damn it all!" The exclamation was rough. Loud. Focused on an empty spot in the air.

"Do this one thing. It won't hurt you or Summer or

anyone else. Do this. Save Wilson Hotels for me. I'll never ask for anything from you again."

For a minute Summer wasn't sure what Lincoln would do. He looked torn into about a million pieces. But he finally nodded. Narrowed his eyes. Murmured, "I'll do it. It's a mistake, but I'll do it. But you never get to call on that debt again."

"Deal." Carter let out a long breath. He leaned over to kiss Summer's cheek. "Thank you so much, Summer. I'm going to call Harold and have him get the contracts changed."

Summer was dazed and a little dizzy as she watched Carter step to the other side of the room and pull out his phone to call the family attorney. She gulped and turned to look at Lincoln.

He was shaking his head and glaring at her with narrowed eyes. "Are you completely insane?"

"I'm not insane. It's fine. What difference does it make if the marriage has your name instead of Carter's? Neither one of them would be a real marriage."

"He's not himself. He's not thinking straight, and clearly neither are you. Surely one of you can see how bad this is. You hate me. And yet you're agreeing to marry me."

"I don't have to like you. Why are you taking it so seriously? I thought you went through life not caring about anything or anyone." She would be a lot more relaxed about this whole thing if Lincoln was acting like his normal obnoxious self.

"I'm taking it seriously because one of us has to." He reached out and gripped her upper arms with his hands. His fingers were tight. Almost too tight. He held her still and met her eyes. "Listen to me, Summer. You tell me right now if you have even the slightest amount of doubt about this. You tell me if even part of you doesn't want to do it. Because I'll call this off right now. I'll tell Carter it's my fault. He'll never know that you were the one to back out. I'll let him hate me forever for it. I'll do it right now. Because there's no way in hell I'm going to marry you unless it's really what you want."

The oddest thing was that, even two minutes ago, she would have had doubts. She would have been worried and not sure if this was a good idea. She couldn't have answered Lincoln's questions truthfully.

But the fact that he was serious—that he would take all the blame on himself to get her out of this situation—eased the anxious twisting in her gut.

Lincoln wasn't a good man. He wasn't a nice one. But he wasn't going to take advantage of her in this.

It was fine. She could do this for Carter and finally do something good with the fortune she'd inherited. She could maybe feel a little less guilty about having so much when other people had so little. Plus it would be over in just a few months.

She nodded. "I'm sure, Lincoln. I want this. If you pull out of it, it has to be because of you. Because I'm all in."

He closed his eyes and let out a long breath. Then he gave her a faintly mocking eyebrow arch. "All right then. I'm in too. But I'm telling you right now it's the biggest mistake you've ever made."

Maybe it was.

But she was going to do it anyway.

2

A WEEK LATER, SUMMER WAS CARRYING AN ARMFUL OF HER clothes up the side stairs in the Wilson mansion to the east wing where her bedroom suite was located.

As long as she'd known them, the Wilson family had lived in an over-the-top Edwardian-style mansion on the lakefront in one of the two large gated communities in town, not far from the marina and country club. It was prime property in Green Valley, and Mr. and Mrs. Wilson had refused to sell it, even after the financial downturn of their company. Carter had moved out to go to college and grad school, but when he returned to town to work for the company, he'd moved back in with his folks.

Lincoln had been renting a loft apartment above his bar ever since he'd broken ties with his family, but he'd moved into the mansion a few days ago after they'd decided no one was going to believe their marriage was legitimate if he and Summer weren't living under the same roof.

Summer wasn't going to do a full move-in. She was only going to be married to Lincoln for a few months—for as short a time as possible, as far as she was concerned—so there was no reason to move more than the clothes she would need and her personal items. But she didn't want to give her trustee any grounds for doubting the nature of her marriage, so both she and Lincoln would live in the mansion with Carter and his mother for the (short) duration of their marriage.

She still couldn't really believe this was happening. She was going to marry Lincoln Wilson, whom she'd slapped just last week. Who'd made her so angry she'd actually thrown up. Who'd spent years exasperating and infuriating her. Who was as obnoxious as a man could be.

What the hell was she thinking?

She'd had more than her share of sleepless nights since she'd agreed to Carter's proposition in which she'd reasoned herself out of the stupid decision. It made no sense. She was letting Carter take advantage of her love and loyalty. She was going to live to regret it.

But every morning when she woke up and prepared to tell Carter she'd changed her mind, she remembered all the years he'd spent working for his father, struggling futilely to earn his respect and prove he was worthwhile.

His father had died before Carter had ever gotten any kind of affirmation that his father had even loved him. This acquisition—saving his family business—was the only thing he had left. The last remaining gesture.

She wasn't going to take it away from him.

It would be fine. Lincoln had been less annoying than usual for the past week. He'd kept mostly to himself, and Summer had only talked to him in the company of other people as they made plans for the marriage. It was all set. They had the marriage license. They would get married at the courthouse tomorrow. They'd announce to Green Valley that they fell madly in love and married on a whim. A few months from now, they'd fulfill every expectation of their friends and acquaintances when they fell out of love and got divorced as all the gossip would predict.

It was all good.

There was no problem.

She didn't need to like Lincoln. They wouldn't be forced into any sort of intimate situation or even have to hang out much together.

All they needed to do was get married on paper and make a few public appearances together to confirm their cover.

She could give Carter this gift before she moved on with her life.

Her bedroom was large with high ceilings, polished floors, and beautifully carved crown moldings. One wall was covered with gorgeous dark red embossed wallpaper, setting off the dark wood of the antique bed. She'd always loved this room, and she was happy that Carter had given it to her.

At the moment, every surface was covered by piles of clothes and shoes and accessories dumped out of the baskets and boxes she'd loosely packed them in.

Carter had offered to hire professional movers, but she'd thought that was a ridiculous waste for a few loads of clothes.

Between her, Carter, and Lincoln, they'd carried everything up in ten minutes.

"This is the last of it." Lincoln's voice came from behind her. She turned to see him coming into the room with a laundry basket full of her nightgowns and pajamas. "Carter's parking your car in the garage."

"Okay. Thanks." She smiled at him politely. She'd been

making an effort to act friendly and natural so this arrangement would be easier for both of them.

Lincoln raised his dark eyebrows in a skeptical expression. He looked ridiculously sexy today in a black V-neck shirt and a pair of jeans that fit him exactly right. His hair needed trimming. He hadn't shaved this morning.

"What?" she demanded, her civil smile turning down into a frown.

"I didn't say anything." He pushed over a pile of coats so he could set the basket down on a corner of the bed.

"You didn't have to say anything. You were giving me that look."

The corners of his mouth twitched irrepressibly. "What look?"

"You know what look. That smug, I-know-better-than-you look. In case you weren't aware, it's one of the most obnoxious expressions I've ever seen on a human face."

"Really? That is a claim to fame. Lucky me."

She rolled her eyes and stifled a groan. He obviously wasn't going to tell her what he was thinking, and her asking him would only give him an advantage. To distract herself, she started sorting through the coats he'd pushed aside, hooking a couple of them back on their hangers.

"Have big plans for this little number, do you?"

She turned back at his voice and gasped when she saw he was holding up a pretty black chemise with lace on the straps and neckline. She snatched it out of his hands and shook it out.

"Trying to get the cooties off now?" There was laughter in Lincoln's voice.

She snarled. "I thought you were trying to be good."

"Why did you think that? When have you ever known me to be good?"

"Well, you've been acting a little better than normal for the past week, so I was hoping..." She was still holding the chemise, staring down at it idly.

He reached over to lift her chin and make her meet his eyes. "Never put your hopes in me, Summer. I'll do nothing but disappoint you."

Her breath hitched at the intensity of his held gaze. She clenched her fingers into the silky fabric she held. "I know that," she replied in nothing more than a whisper.

His eyes flickered, and his face transformed back into his typical mocking expression. "But if you ever want to give that lingerie a whirl, I'm your man."

She stepped back and scowled again, the sudden shift in mood disorienting her. "You can't possibly think I'd ever wear this for you."

"Well, no. Obviously not. I'm sure you packed that with visions of wandering the halls in it at night to get a book or a drink of water and *accidently* running into my brother, who will be so blown away by unleashed desire that he carries you to his room for a night of passion."

"Bastard," Summer hissed. She wanted to take a few steps backward since he was invading her personal space again, but as always, that felt like a defeat. She held her position and glared up at him. "Clearly it never occurred to you that I might wear pretty things for myself."

"Oh yeah? So you like to give yourself a real good time?"

Her first instinct was to yell at him. To whirl around and get away. But she must be getting better at holding her own with him because she managed to keep her voice cool as she replied, "Of course I do. It's better than making do with the dubious skills of a man like you."

She'd surprised him. She could see it on his face. But if she'd hoped he would be annoyed or subdued, she was doomed to disappointment. He gave a soft huff of dry amusement, his green eyes softening into something akin to appreciation. "Thank you."

"For what?"

"For that image." He leaned forward and murmured into her ear in a thick voice that made her shiver with pleasure. "Now I can give myself a real good time by imagining you."

She flushed hot and turned back to her coats. "What you do in the privacy of your room is your own business. As long as you know it's never going to happen in real life."

"You say that now, but one day you might realize the truth."

She turned back toward him with a jerk of her head. "What truth?"

He gave her an almost wicked smile. "That there's nothing in the world hotter than hate sex. And there's no one in the world you hate more than me."

SUMMER MARRIED Lincoln Wilson the following day on her lunch break.

It was a quick, no-nonsense ceremony. Carter was present, as was Summer's best female friend, Nona. Summer went back to work afterward, feeling strange and unsettled and oddly incomplete.

But it was done. She was married. And they were a step

closer to being done with this ridiculous scheme so she could start her real life again.

That evening after work, she returned to the Wilson mansion, which was going to be her home for the next few months.

Lincoln wasn't home. Since he was a bartender, his shifts were in the evenings. It worked out well because it meant she wouldn't have to see him very often. Things would be better that way.

She'd had heated, restless daydreams all last night prompted by that one sexy conversation she'd had with him in the bedroom while she'd unpacked. The less time she spent with him, the better.

Carter was getting home at the same time she did, and she found him at the bar in the living room, pouring himself a glass of bourbon.

"Drinking already?" she asked, smiling at him as she approached.

He looked tired. He'd taken off his suit jacket and loosened his tie. "One of those days."

"Is everything all right?" She wasn't a big drinker, so she shook her head as he gestured toward the bar as a wordless offer to pour her a drink.

"It's fine. It's just been a long week. And I'm starting to feel kind of bad."

"Bad about what?"

He met her eyes with his sober brown ones. "About bullying you into this thing."

"No! You didn't bully me into it, Carter. I knew what I was doing, and I agreed."

"I know you did. But you agreed because you felt sorry for

me. Right? I guilted you into it."

"Not on purpose. I mean, yeah, I felt bad for you. But I also knew this would help. And it's not really that big a deal. I was going to marry you for the same reasons. Why shouldn't I do it with Lincoln?"

"Because Lincoln's an ass. He's always teasing you and flirting with you. I know it makes you uncomfortable."

Summer licked her lips, trying to find the best words to respond. "Well, yeah, he is kind of an ass. But I'm getting used to him, and the teasing isn't a big deal. It's just his way. I don't take it personally. It's hardly a marriage at all. I won't have to see him very much."

"He'll be living right next door to you."

To protect their cover, Lincoln took the bedroom that connected to Summer's by a private door, just in case anyone wandered through the house and questioned the legitimacy of their marriage. "Who cares about that? I'm never going to unlock that door. It won't be any different than if he lived on the other side of the house next to you. It's fine, Carter. It really is. I can put up with a jerk for a few months. I want to do this. I want to help you."

He held her gaze. His expression softened. "Thank you, Summer. I'll never be able to repay you."

She gave him a soft hug. "You won't have to. That's what it means to be friends."

"Mom wants to have a brunch for the two of you. As a sort of wedding announcement and celebration combined. She's thinking two weeks from Sunday. Is that okay? She's got a trip planned for the south of France after that, so she needs to get the brunch in quickly."

Summer nodded. "That's fine. As long as you think we can get Lincoln to behave himself for a few hours."

"I can. He will."

Something about his expression prompted Summer's curiosity. "Why does he owe you?"

"What?"

"Lincoln. Why does he owe you? It must be something big for him to agree to this. What did he do? Why does he owe you?"

Carter shook his head. "It doesn't matter."

"It matters to me. I care about you, and I'm involved in this. What did he do?" She was almost holding her breath. She had no idea why the answer to this question mattered to her so much.

Lincoln must have done something truly terrible to owe such a huge debt to his brother.

"I promised him I wouldn't tell you. I'm sorry, Summer. I can't."

Her shoulders slumped slightly, but she didn't argue anymore. After all, a promise was a promise. And Carter would never go back on his word.

She wouldn't even want him to.

"All right. I won't pester you about it."

"I'm going to owe you big at the end of this thing," Carter said, raising a hand to touch her hair. "You know that, right?"

Summer flashed a smile. "Yes, I know that. But I doubt I'll ever ask you to collect. I'm doing it because I want to. Because you've been family to me when I didn't have anyone else."

This time Carter was the one who hugged her. He held her in his arms for a long time.

SUMMER HAD a quiet evening with Carter, eating sandwiches in front of the television and then going to bed early. She slept deeply and woke up disoriented in the middle of the night.

She knew vaguely where she was, but it was dark in the room and she needed to pee, so she rolled out of bed and stumbled in the general direction of the bathroom attached to her room.

She'd mostly finished unpacking, but she'd left a box of books and a laundry basket full of purses in the middle of the floor to put up the next day. Unfortunately, she'd left them directly on her route to the bathroom.

She tripped on the laundry basket. Since it wasn't heavy, it moved when her foot connected, so it wasn't enough to make her completely lose her balance. But it tripped her up enough for her to take a few awkward steps. One of those steps was right into the box of books.

Her foot got caught in the box and she lost it. Her ankle twisted. Her body collapsed. She fell hard. She grabbed for the edge of the dresser, catching herself before she hit her head but wrenching her shoulder as she did. The corner of the dresser jammed into her upper left arm, slicing down a few inches before she caught herself. And her knee slammed one of the drawer pulls.

She let go and allowed herself to slide slowly to the floor, her mind momentarily numbed by the shock and pain. After a minute, she tried to assess her situation.

She was okay. She could move. Nothing was broken. She'd cut up the soft flesh on the upper part of her left arm.

Her ankle was twisted, so it hurt but not enough for even a sprain. And she'd bruised her knee.

She stood up slowly, relaxing as the adrenaline subsided. She was in some pain and she was bleeding at her knee and upper arm, but there was no crisis here. She could walk. She wouldn't need to ask for help.

It was upsetting to fall and hurt herself like this, but since she could have knocked herself unconscious on the edge of the dresser, she wasn't about to complain about a few minor injuries.

She limped into her bathroom and checked the medicine cabinet and under the sink. There was extra toilet paper there and a couple of spare boxes of tissues but nothing else. They'd obviously cleared everything out for her before she moved in.

She needed bandages for her cuts. And she hadn't thought to bring first aid supplies with her. She peed and wiped away some of the blood with tissues. Then she went out to the hall, looking in both directions.

It was mostly dark—with just a faint cast of light from the stairwell at the end of the hall. She knew there were bandages in the bathrooms downstairs. She'd seen them there. But blood was dripping down her arm, and her ankle hurt, and she was still kind of shaky from the fall. She didn't want to walk all the way down there if she didn't have to.

She turned on the hall light and saw that Lincoln's bedroom door was wide open. She walked over to peer inside and saw it was dark.

He wasn't there. He was still working. She had no idea what time it was, but he always worked really late. He wasn't home yet.

Maybe he had first aid stuff in his bathroom.

Deciding it was worth checking, she walked into his room. It was beautifully furnished like hers was, and he hadn't yet unpacked. A suitcase was open on the floor, over-flowing with clothes. There was a pile of books on his night-stand and a laptop on the small desk in the corner.

She was tempted to snoop, but she wasn't foolish enough to do so. His shift at the bar might have ended, and he could appear at any time. Instead, she hurried to his attached bath-room and searched for bandages.

Nothing. The shelves and drawers were just as empty as hers.

With a frustrated sigh, she got out of there and limped downstairs to the big bathroom near the kitchen.

She turned on the light and bent over to check one of the drawers under the sink, where she remembered seeing first aid supplies in the past. She was reaching for a box of bandages when a familiar male voice sounded from behind her.

"Well, it was a good plan. I'll give you that. It's just your bad luck that the wrong brother happened to find you all rumpled and sexy in the middle of the night. I'm a little disappointed that you're not wearing that hot little black number, but your ass does look very fine in those pajamas."

Summer was so surprised by the voice that she gasped and jerked up to a standing position. Given the way her life was going lately, it was no surprise that her abrupt motion caused her head to slam against the granite edge of the sink surround.

"Damn it!" She held on to her head as she managed to stand up, her vision momentarily blurred by the pain.

She was wearing pink cotton pajama shorts and a little white tank top. She wasn't dressed for an encounter with Lincoln Wilson. Especially with blood running down her arm and leg.

When she turned around, she saw he was giving her a smug little smile, his eyes running up and down her body. But then he must have gotten a better look at her condition. His expression changed. "Shit. What the hell happened?"

"I fell." Her voice cracked. Her head and her ankle and her arm and her knee all hurt. "I was looking for Band-Aids."

"Did you fall down the fucking stairs?" Lincoln was dressed in black trousers and an untucked charcoal gray button-up. He looked sleek and modern and wide-awake and sexy as hell, and he was the last thing she wanted to see right now. "You're a mess. Sit down. I'll fix you up."

"I don't need you to fix me up." She swiped a stray tear away, hoping he didn't see it.

He saw it. Of course he did. He shook his head and gave her a faintly annoyed eye roll. "Sit your ass down. You're about to get bloodstains on a thousand-dollar rug."

Summer gasped and looked down at the bathmat under her feet. It was thick and pure white. Blood was slowly trickling down her shin. She sat on the closed toilet and used her hand to wipe the stream of blood from her skin before it dripped to the floor. "Does that rug really cost a thousand dollars?"

"I haven't a clue. Knowing my mom, it's possible. But I mostly just wanted to get you to stop arguing." He was smirking again as he pulled supplies out of the first aid drawer. He set them on the floor near her feet and then grabbed a soft white washcloth from beside the sink, getting it wet.

Because she was still kind of blurry, it took her a minute to realize what he was doing. "Wait! Don't use that to—" She broke off because it was too late.

Lincoln had leaned over and was mopping the blood off her left arm with the expensive white washcloth. He knelt down on the floor as he worked, bringing him far too close to her.

She was silent as he wiped the blood off her upper arm and then cleaned up her knee. His eyes were focused on his task. His body was big and firm and fit and solid. He smelled like liquor and night air and maybe the slightest hint of spicy aftershave. She held herself very still.

"Doesn't look too bad," he murmured, inspecting the cut on her arm. "You don't need stitches or anything. It's bruised though."

"It's fine." She was relieved that her voice was low and even since she was feeling shakier than ever.

She really wanted to touch his face. His thick, dark hair. The fabric of his shirt.

He spread antibiotic salve on her cut before he pulled a couple of bandages out of the box. "Let me guess. You were out on your midnight vigil, hoping to run into Carter for an accidental seduction, and you were so wrapped up in daydreams about him that you missed a stair." He unwrapped the bandages and then leaned closer to apply them to her arm.

She narrowed her eyes with a familiar surge of anger. The stupidest thing was that she still wanted to touch him.

When she didn't reply, he looked up at her face. They

were only inches away from each other. "I guessed it right, didn't I?"

"No," she gritted out. "You did not."

He was silent for a moment. He lowered himself on his knees when he finished with her arm and turned his attention to her leg. He wiped up a little more blood and then gently rubbed on the salve.

She gazed down at him as he worked. She couldn't help it. It was so strange for him to tend to her in this way. His fingers were touching her bare skin. It felt intimate.

Far too intimate.

He flashed her a quick, searching look. "So what did happen?"

She chewed on her upper lip for a few seconds before she relented. "I was going to the bathroom, and I tripped on a stupid box of books. I fell against the dresser."

His arched his eyebrows. "Are you in a habit of taking such disastrous tumbles?"

"No. It was dark, and I'm not used to the room yet."

Lincoln nodded and used two bandages to cover the cut on her knee. "Did you hurt anything else?"

"I twisted my ankle a little, but it's not bad." She wriggled her foot slightly to confirm that her words were true.

He reached for her foot, gently turning it in different directions, watching her face as he did.

"I told you it's not bad. It's not sprained."

Both his warm hands were holding her bare foot. He was on his knees on the floor in front of her. Their eyes met and held. She couldn't look away. She twisted her trembling hands in her lap and resisted the urge to touch him.

He swallowed. She saw it in his throat. Then he let go of her foot with a strange, slow caution.

He rose to his feet and offered her a hand. She took it, letting him help her to her feet.

They stared at each other some more, standing together in the middle of the silent bathroom. She could hear herself breathing. Too quickly. Almost raggedly.

What the hell was wrong with her? She didn't even like this man.

She jerked her gaze away, staring instead at the floor.

"Well, I've done my good deed for the night," Lincoln said lightly, taking a step back from her. "I can now sleep the sleep of the righteous."

She snorted, his wry tone dragging her out of the shaky intensity of the moment before. "You've never slept the sleep of the righteous in your life."

"That is sadly true. My brother inherited any shred of righteousness that exists in our genes. He's the saint. I'm the sinner."

She gave him an impatient look.

"What's that look for?" He was once more brimming with his dry, almost playful arrogance. "Do you deny that I'm the sinner of the family?"

"Of course I don't deny it. Just like it's impossible to deny how good a man Carter is."

"Exactly. He's a good man. And I'm a bad one. We're in full agreement on this issue. Why do you insist on arguing with everything I say?"

"Because everything you say is either wrong or obnoxious or completely inappropriate. If you'd change what you say, I wouldn't argue with you all the time."

He laughed, low and soft and irresistible. His vivid eyes were oddly soft.

She was so deeply drawn to him in that moment that Summer decided it was well past time for her to make an escape. "Okay. Thanks for your help. I'm going to bed now."

"Next time, you should do your midnight wanderings in the west wing. You'll have better luck encountering Carter there."

"I wasn't trying to run into Carter." She pushed past him to leave the bathroom.

"Sure you weren't." His smug voice followed her down the hall, but she didn't turn around.

3
———

Two weeks later, Summer came downstairs at just before seven on a Friday morning and was surprised to see Lincoln lounging in a chair at the head of the table in the breakfast room.

The breakfast room was small and cozy with casual maple furniture and big windows that let in the morning sun. For as long as Summer could remember, the Wilson family had eaten breakfast there and never set foot in the room otherwise.

Lincoln was reading something on his phone, and he didn't glance up as she came in. He wore trousers and a dress shirt. He didn't smell like whiskey, and he'd obviously just shaved.

Summer's stomach clenched, and she told herself it was because a clean and awake Lincoln wasn't what she wanted to encounter first thing the morning.

It wasn't because she was glad to see him.

She was dressed for work in heels, man-style trousers,

and a cute pink top. She didn't let her eyes linger on Lincoln as she made her way to the pot of coffee on the sideboard.

"Mornin', sunshine," Lincoln drawled, still focused on his phone.

She curled up her lip and shot him an annoyed glare.

Lincoln finally raised his eyes from his phone, just in time to see her expression. "No good-morning kiss for your husband this morning?"

"My husband gets what he deserves, which in this case is to have his obnoxiousness ignored." She set her mug of coffee down at her normal place, which happened to be right beside Lincoln. "Didn't you work last night?"

"I did."

"So what are you doing up bright and early this morning? Don't you normally sleep until noon?"

"If I had my choice, that's what I'd be doing today too, but duty calls."

"What duty?" She put a toasted English muffin and a boiled egg on her plate and sat down.

"Brotherly duties." He twitched his eyebrows. "Sadly, I haven't been called on for any husbandly duties yet, but I'll be happy to provide any services you require."

Her cheeks warmed at the obvious innuendo in his words and look, but she'd gotten better at dealing with Lincoln over the past weeks, so she was able to keep her expression cool and composed. "Your only husbandly duty is not to drive your wife crazy with your attitude, and you certainly haven't managed to accomplish that."

He leaned closer with an exaggerated seductiveness that was almost playful. "Just how crazy do I drive you?"

She tried—she really tried—not to smile. It was never a

good idea to encourage him to act this way. But he was so brazen. So ridiculously over-the-top. So clever.

It was impossible not to find him just a little funny.

He relaxed back into his chair. "Gotcha," he murmured with a pleased smile over the rim of his coffee cup.

"You do not have me. I wasn't laughing."

"You were trying not to, but I caught a hint of a smile. I knew you'd come around to my irresistible appeal eventually."

"Any irresistibility you possess is only in your own mind. The only thing I have trouble resisting when I'm around you is giving you a smack across the face."

"One time you didn't even resist that." He rubbed his cheek where she'd slapped him on the day of his father's funeral.

She closed her eyes and let out a breath. "I know that. I said I was sorry. I never should have hit you."

He gave a little shrug. "I deserved it. And probably a lot more."

Summer searched his face and couldn't see anything there that doubted his sincerity. So she nodded in acknowledgment and changed the subject. "What brotherly duty do you have this morning?"

"I've got to go through a bunch of stuff with Carter about the hotel deal."

"I thought that was already worked out. Is everything okay?"

"Yes. But you know Carter. He's all stressed out about it, so he wants to make sure all his ducks are in a row. Thus I have to make do with just four hours of sleep so I can get to the office bright and early."

"Bright and early? Carter has probably been there for an hour already."

"Well, there are limits to how bright and how early I can do. I didn't get home until two."

"You have to work again tonight?"

"Of course."

"Why did you become a bartender?"

He was finishing his coffee, but he slanted her a questioning look as he lowered the mug. Like he was trying to determine if her question was serious or not. It was, and he must have seen that because he replied lightly, "Just kind of fell into it. I never finished college. I'm not trained for anything. I wasn't going to live off my dad anymore, and I needed a job. A friend got me a job behind the bar at Milhouse. I was good at it. People liked me. So I stuck with it."

"Plus your dad hated it."

"That too." He met her gaze with a soft smile in his eyes. "Just an added benefit."

"You could still finish college."

"Eh."

"What do you mean, *eh*? Why shouldn't you?"

"That's not the question. The question is why should I. What would it do for me? I don't need a college degree to serve drinks."

"But you don't have to be a bartender all your life." She was getting into the conversation and becoming earnest. Sincerity was her normal state of mind, but she didn't often risk it around Lincoln. With him, she usually had to stay on guard. "I mean, you're not *that* old. You could finish college and have an entirely different career if you want."

"What makes you think I want that?" He sounded half teasing but not entirely so.

"I don't know. What do I know? It's just that you don't really seem happy. Maybe doing something else would make you happier." Her eyes were wide, and her voice sounded worried, and she felt a flutter of fear that her genuine attempt to help him would be met with a slammed door.

He stared at her for a long time, his eyes looking a lighter green than normal in the morning sunshine. His lips were slightly parted. She couldn't really read his expression, but the closest she could come was surprised. "I think I'm as happy as I can get," he murmured at last.

"But that's ridiculous. Why would you say that? Why couldn't you be happier?"

He stared some more. His body felt tenser than normal. "I... I don't know," he breathed.

She gazed back at him with a sudden urge to reach out and touch him. Hold his hand. Stroke his arm. Press her palm against his heart.

She managed to resist those ludicrous urges and not do anything to embarrass herself. She couldn't speak though. Any words were caught in her throat.

They were silent for a long time until she finally remembered she should eat her breakfast. She licked her lips and focused down on her plate. What was she thinking? She should never try to have a real conversation with Lincoln. The best she could hope for from him was teasing without too harsh a bite.

They sat without talking for a couple of minutes until she dared to shoot a quick look up at his face.

He was watching her with something between curiosity and skepticism.

She rolled her eyes. "What?"

"What, what?"

"Why are you looking at me like that?"

"You're the only other person in the room. And you're certainly the prettiest thing in the room. What else would I look at?"

"Why do you do that?"

"Do what?"

"Say things that you know will annoy me."

"Why does it annoy you that I say you're pretty?"

The question surprised her so much she answered it honestly. "Because you don't mean it. You're just saying it to rile me up."

His eyebrows shot upward. "I do too mean it. How can you think I don't?"

"Because I'm not... I'm not... I mean, I'm not bad to look at, but I'm not..."

The teasing in his eyes faded as he said, "I've never known anyone prettier than you. That's the truth. I've always thought so. You shouldn't be surprised that I'd say it."

She flushed hot and dropped her eyes to her plate. Her blood throbbed with excitement and pleasure, but her heart hammered with anxiety. She had no idea how she could possibly respond to what he'd just said, but she could have sworn he was serious.

Did he really think she was pretty? He was so handsome and sexy that he could have any woman he wanted. She couldn't believe he'd be genuinely attracted to her.

"Now I've embarrassed you." His tone was light and mocking again.

She narrowed her eyes into a glare. "I'm not embarrassed."

"Oh yes, you are." He laughed softly as he stood up and leaned over. She was staring up at him in surprise as he brushed a soft kiss against her right cheekbone. "But that's okay. Embarrassment looks good on you."

To her relief, he left the room then, leaving her to a fluttery rush of feelings she really didn't want to entertain.

～

ON SUNDAY MORNING, Mrs. Wilson threw Lincoln and Summer a wedding brunch.

For the past two weeks, Summer had been inundated with calls, visits, and messages from friends and acquaintances who wanted to hear all about her surprise marriage to Lincoln Wilson. They'd already agreed on a simple backstory for their relationship. They'd started spending time together after his father was diagnosed with cancer. Sparks ignited. Feelings grew. They fell hopelessly in love and didn't want to waste any time after his father died, so they eloped.

Anyone who knew Summer would realize this was out of character for her. She was always careful. Reflective. Safe in her choices. But she pretended to have been swept away by Lincoln's passion and impulsiveness, so the story was convincing enough.

She could see how it might happen. Lincoln had the kind of magnetic personality and pure animal heat that could lead even cautious people to do things they wouldn't ordinarily do.

So far, she'd been met by both delighted surprise and sly excitement. But no disbelief.

No one had any trouble believing that quiet, shy Summer Cray (and the enormous fortune she'd inherited) would get swept off her feet by sexy, dangerous Lincoln Wilson. Evidently she made for a convincing cliché.

It bugged her a little, but not enough to act on. She certainly wasn't silly enough to not take advantage of assumptions that were working in their favor—no matter how annoying those assumptions happened to be.

So on Sunday morning, she put on a pretty cream-colored dress (since she looked terrible in pure white). The dress had a sweetheart neckline, lace sleeves, and a soft drape that flattered her curvy figure. She looked good. Innocent. Rather old-fashioned. Mrs. Wilson would definitely approve.

Lincoln would probably laugh.

She didn't care what Lincoln thought of her appearance, but she felt uncomfortably bridal as she put on pearl earrings and a necklace. Afraid she was running late, she came out to the hallway still trying to hook the matching bracelet.

She hadn't yet fastened it when she saw a man approaching in an expensive medium-gray suit and silver tie. She blinked and then blinked again as she realized the man was Lincoln.

"What are you wearing?" she gasped, running her eyes up and down his lean body in the uncharacteristic clothes. "I didn't think you owned a suit!"

He gave her a slight sneer. "It's Carter's. I was told in no uncertain terms that if I didn't wear a suit, I'd be a disgrace to the Wilson name and could never show my face at home again. So here I am. Looking like an idiot."

"You don't look like an idiot. You look good." She couldn't stop staring at him. There was something incongruous and unsettling about him in Carter's suit. "You just don't look like yourself."

"Well, I'm sure that's a good thing, as far as you're concerned." He glanced down at the bracelet she was still holding around her wrist. "You need help with that?"

"Oh. Yeah. Sure." She lifted her hand as he reached for the bracelet and stared down at his strong, agile fingers as they fastened the clasp. He did it slowly. Carefully. Almost delicately. And for some reason it made her tremble.

He raised his eyes to her face when he'd finished. She was still holding her hand up like an idiot.

They stared at each other for a moment before she remembered to drop her hand. She forced a casual smile. "Ready to pretend like we're crazy in love?"

"I am if you are."

"I'm not sure I'm ever going to be ready for this. I hate to be the center of attention. And it doesn't help that this whole thing is just a ruse." She felt a swell of familiar fear—the way she always did when she had to take center stage in a social setting.

His eyes searched her face briefly. Then he leaned over and murmured into her ear. "You'll do fine. Just pretend I'm Carter."

It took a moment for the words to register. When they did, she sucked in an outraged gasp and gave him a little shove away from her. "Asshole."

He smiled. Almost fondly. "There you go. Now you're ready."

She had to fight not to scowl and jerk away from him as they made their way through the hall to the central stairway of the mansion. A lot of the guests were already gathered in the marble-floored foyer, and they all turned to smile up at the newly married couple.

Lincoln twitched his dark eyebrows at her and offered his arm.

With a smile pasted on her lips and a cold glare in her eyes, she took it. Guests applauded as they descended the stairs.

The whole thing was a ridiculous sham, and Lincoln's smug smirk made everything worse. She was too annoyed with him to be nervous, so she supposed that was a good thing.

When they were down the stairs, she was tempted to let go of Lincoln's arm, but that probably wouldn't fit her image of a head-over-heels-in-love new bride. So she kept clinging, wishing his arm wasn't quite so firm under the fabric of his sleeve. Wishing he didn't smell quite so good.

They greeted their smiling guests as they wandered through the ornate space. Most of them were people she'd known all her life since the Green Valley community was stable and rather ingrown. When they'd reached the far wall, Lincoln picked a small bouquet of pale pink peonies from an antique console table and offered it to her with a flourish that made observers smile and giggle. His green eyes were laughing at her.

She accepted the bouquet, holding it up to her nose and

trying to look like she adored Lincoln instead of wanting to yank that pleased smile right off his face.

The brunch was a formal, plated meal, complete with professional servers and an open bar. There were about forty people present, and Summer and Lincoln had to sit together at the head table.

The food and drink were delicious, but Summer didn't enjoy the meal. It went on forever, and she soon grew tired of explaining how she and Lincoln fell in love and how, yes, it was an impulsive decision but they were very happy.

When the meal was finally over, guests lingered, drinking and chatting and asking inappropriately intrusive questions about Summer and Lincoln's history and plans for the future.

Summer was a true introvert, and so she was always exhausted after parties. But she was more worn out than usual when one o'clock came and went and the brunch went on. There was a table full of wedding gifts, but they weren't going to open them at the party. There was nothing left to do at the brunch. Just wait until people finally left.

Lincoln was schmoozing like a master, but it was clear he was going through the whole routine with tongue firmly in cheek. Ironic amusement glittered in his eyes, growing more or less bitter, depending on how much he respected the people he was talking to. Very few of them he liked. She could see that very clearly. But some he didn't hate as much as others.

Summer finally had to give herself a break by slipping away to the bathroom. She needed to pee anyway, but mostly she just wanted to take a few deep breaths away from the crowd and recover her equilibrium. She'd put her hair in a pretty, soft bun at the nape of her neck, and she used the opportunity to smooth down a few strands that had slipped out and were framing her face. Otherwise, she still looked nice. And she hadn't even spilled anything on her dress.

She was on her way back from the bathroom when she ran into Mariana Brubaker, a gorgeous, snobbish former classmate who had always made Summer feel plain and mousy. Mariana gushed with fake, condescending excitement about Summer's elopement.

Summer had to fight to keep a smile on her face. She knew cattiness when she was faced with it, and Mariana was as catty as it got.

"I was pretty surprised to hear about it," Mariana continued, that false, toothy smile never wavering on her perfectly made-up mouth. "But after I thought about it, I decided it made sense. I'm sure Lincoln is happy about your inheritance since he wasn't getting anything from his father. And you've probably never been with anyone as good in bed as he is."

Summer blinked, momentarily astonished by the turn from pointed undercurrents to overt meanness.

Mariana laughed and gave her a pat on her shoulder. "Don't look so dumbfounded, Summer. You knew I had a fling with him, didn't you? The man is sex personified. That's not enough for me, but everyone is different, aren't we?"

Her head throbbed and her eyes blurred over as she processed the weaponized pleasantries. She wasn't like Lincoln. Or like Savannah Emerson. Or like people who could always think of something clever to say.

She couldn't say anything at all.

Since the only thing that came to her to do was to claw lines down Mariana's face, she turned around and walked away. She was shaking as she reached Lincoln, who was holding a half-drunk glass of scotch and leaning against a wall in the living room where everyone had spilled into from the dining room. He looked relaxed, which made sense since he was chatting with his brother and Lance Carlyle—two people he didn't despise.

When Summer came to his side, he wrapped an arm around her. No doubt as part of their pose as a romantic couple. He must have felt her shaking, however, because he straightened up and tilted his head down to murmur into her ear, "What's the matter?"

She shook her head and forced a smile up at him.

Lincoln frowned and turned toward the two other men. "Give us a minute, will you?"

"Lincoln, there's nothing—" Summer broke off because Carter and Lance were already backing off. Carter was watching her in concern. She scowled up at Lincoln. "We don't need a minute."

"Tell me what's wrong."

"Nothing's wrong."

"Do you really think I can't see what's right in front of my face? You're shaking. Someone upset you. Who was it?" He had her backed up against a wall, holding her in place with the position of his body although he wasn't touching her at all.

She knew Lincoln well enough to know there wasn't any use in arguing with him when he was in this mood. He was ridiculously stubborn. "I'm not that upset. It wasn't a big deal. I just had a run-in with Mariana, and she made me mad."

"Mariana Brubaker? I'm not surprised she made you mad. She seems to have a mission of making herself feel superior to everyone else. She's not worth getting upset about."

His unconcerned tone did nothing to quiet her uproarious feelings. "Well, she's evidently worth your screwing."

Lincoln's eyebrows lifted. "What?"

"You thought she was worth screwing. Didn't you?"

"She told you that?"

"Yes, she told me that. She threw it in my face."

He was frowning now, his relaxed unconcern finally fading. He was still standing way too close to her. He'd planted a hand on the wall beside her, and his head was tilted toward hers. "And it really upset you that much? I had sex with her once. More than ten years ago now. She wanted more, and I didn't. It was a mistake. I've made a lot of mistakes. I can't take any of them back. I don't want you to get upset every time one of my mistakes rears its ugly head and drops itself into your lap."

For some reason his low, sober voice was distressing her more than anything else. She was still trembling helplessly, and her throat ached with emotion. "I'm not upset that you slept with her. Your sex life is your own business."

"Well, you're upset about something. Tell me what it is."

She swallowed and then swallowed again. Her mind wasn't working well enough to come up with a safe response, so she ended up telling him the truth. "She made me feel... small. Like I'm not worth marrying for anything but my money. I know that's what she was trying to do, and I know it's not true, but I can't always help but... get upset by it."

He stood still for a long time, his eyes focused on her face. It looked like he was thinking, processing, making sense of something that didn't make sense to Summer. When he finally spoke, his voice was slightly raspy. "She said I was just marrying you for the money?"

"Yes. And it's true, right?"

"It doesn't matter what's true. Because what's not true is that money is the only reason a man would want to marry you." Before Summer could wrap her mind around what he'd just said, he continued, "We can do something about that. Do you want to?"

"Do I want... what?" Her knees weren't exactly working at the moment, so she reached out to hold on to the lapels of his suit jacket for some extra support.

He stepped into her. "We can make it clear I'm not marrying you just for the money."

"How?" she breathed.

He leaned down so his mouth was a whisper away from hers. "Like this." Then he kissed her.

The kiss was gentle at first. Almost questioning. His lips lightly brushed against hers and then softly surrounded her upper lip. When a surge of pleasure caused her to cling to the back of his neck with both hands, his mouth pressed against hers more firmly.

He lifted one hand to span the side of her neck, holding her head in place as he deepened the kiss.

Maybe because her emotions were already so unsettled, but the kiss completely consumed her. Pleasure and excitement and a thrilling kind of fear flooded her veins, heated her skin, throbbed with her racing heartbeat. She pressed herself against him as his tongue teased between her lips. She couldn't help but open for him.

It was a mistake. As soon as his tongue got into the action, the pleasure turned to bone-deep arousal. And she couldn't be aroused. Not right now. Not in the middle of a wedding brunch.

Not by Lincoln Wilson.

She jerked her mouth away and hid her face against his shoulder. She wanted to pull away from him completely, but she couldn't. He was supposed to be her beloved husband.

Lincoln followed her lead. He didn't pursue the kiss. He wrapped one arm around her and held her in what must look like a hug to observers. "Y'okay?" he murmured thickly. Right against her ear.

"Yes." She found the will to straighten up and pull away from him. Fortunately, her legs managed to support her. "I understand what you were trying to do just now."

His face was slightly flushed. Tense. His eyes were almost urgent. "Do you?"

"Yes. You were trying to prove to Mariana and everyone else that we're really in love. But please don't do that again without asking first."

He nodded. "Understood."

She turned away from him since his intense expression was too confusing, too unsettling. The first thing she saw on turning was Carter. He was watching her. Frowning in what looked like confused concern.

She gulped and dropped her eyes.

He didn't understand what he'd just witnessed. And that made perfect sense.

Because Summer didn't understand it herself.

THE FINAL GUESTS left at almost three o'clock in the afternoon. Four and a half hours of challenging socializing and being the center of attention was definitely Summer's limit, and she barely had enough energy to thank Mrs. Wilson for throwing the brunch and to give Carter a hug before she limped upstairs to change clothes and collapse on her bed.

She was still lying sprawled out in yoga pants and an oversized T-shirt and with her favorite velvety brown throw over her legs twenty minutes later when there was a knock on her bedroom door.

It was probably Carter. He'd been quiet for most of the brunch, and she suspected he was worried about her. She didn't care who it was. She wasn't about to get up to open the door herself. "Come in!"

The door opened and a man stepped in.

It wasn't Carter.

She lifted her head and blinked in the direction of Lincoln's familiar form. Despite the fact that his face was shadowed because it was light in the hall but not in her room and he was the same height and build as his younger brother with the same thick brown hair, she could tell the difference immediately. Not just by the fact that Lincoln's hair was a little too long but also by something in his stance. The way he held his shoulders. His head.

She didn't need to see his face to know it was Lincoln.

"What?" she demanded.

"Can I come in?"

"Yeah. Sure. What's going on?" She managed to heave herself into a sitting position.

"Nothing. Just checking on you."

She frowned, confused and rattled by this unexpected gesture. "I'm fine. Too much fake smiling for me. Socializing tires me out."

"I know it does. That's not what I was checking on." He was unusually serious as he came over and sat down on the bed beside her. "I'm sorry I kissed you without asking first."

She was so surprised her mouth dropped open. "Oh."

"I wasn't thinking. I never think." His face twisted in a way that proved he was unsettlingly serious about this. "I usually know when a woman wants me to kiss her, and it felt like you…" He shook his head fiercely. "But we're in a weird situation here. I should have asked first."

"No, it's fine, Lincoln. Seriously. I wasn't… wasn't ready for it, but it didn't feel like you were… It's fine. Thanks for the apology, but we're fine."

His expression relaxed into his normal little smile. The one that was usually so annoying but was somehow appealing just now. "Okay. Good. I'll ask before I do it again."

She couldn't help but return his smile.

It felt like she needed to raise a few defenses against him. He was managing to wheedle his way into her affections even though she knew how dangerous that would be. So she said, "I don't think you'll need to do it again."

"Why not?"

"Because we don't have to go around kissing all the time just to convince the world we're really married. The wedding rings should do the trick just fine." She glanced down at her left hand, vaguely surprised to see the wedding band there. It was pretty. Platinum. Engraved with a simple pattern. She didn't have an engagement ring since she and Lincoln hadn't had an engagement, and it had been silly to waste the money for a few months of a marriage.

She shifted her eyes over to Lincoln's left hand, which was

resting on the bed between them. He had a matching ring. Larger but made as a set with hers.

Seeing it on his hand made her feel strange and fluttery. She lifted her eyes to discover he was watching her.

She cleared her throat. "So kissing probably isn't necessary."

"I don't know. There are a lot of obtuse people in Green Valley. They might need a lot of convincing. We should probably kiss a lot to make sure no one suspects."

She laughed. She couldn't help it.

He was obviously pleased with her response. His eyes warmed and he leaned toward her. "And we should probably do some practicing—just to make sure our kissing performance is at the top of its game. What do you say? You want to practice right now?"

He was so obviously teasing that she wasn't even offended. She was still laughing as she gave him a gentle shove backward. "No, we're not going to practice."

He was grinning as he stood up. He'd changed into jeans and a black T-shirt, and he looked way too good in it. More himself. Somehow even sexier than he'd been in Carter's suit. "You sure? We wouldn't even need to do it for practice since we're pretty good at it already. We could do it just for fun."

"Kissing you is not fun, Lincoln." That wasn't at all true, but she could hardly admit to how much she'd enjoyed their kiss earlier.

"You shouldn't lie to your devoted husband." He was heading for the open door of the bedroom, and he said the words over his shoulder, flashing her another smile.

"I'm not lying, you arrogant jackass!" For good measure, she tossed one of the throw pillows on her bed in his direction. Her aim was good, and it bounced off his lower back and onto the floor.

He laughed as he leaned over and tossed the pillow back. It landed neatly on the bed just beside her. "This brutal attack on my person is clearly the sign for me to make a speedy retreat. But my offer stands. We can have all the fun you want." He twitched his eyebrows from the doorway. "Just say the word."

"Get out of here, and take your overinflated ego and your obnoxious smirk with you as you go!" There was laughter in her voice, and she knew he would hear it.

He was chuckling as he disappeared down the hall.

She was about to relax back on her bed when another male figure appeared in her doorway. For a moment she thought Lincoln had returned, but it wasn't him.

It was Carter. He said, "Hey."

"Hey. Come on in. What are you doing?"

"Just checking on you."

She smiled at him as he approached the bed and patted the mattress beside her to invite him to sit. "I'm fine. I don't need everyone checking on me."

"I heard Lincoln in here earlier. So he beat me to it, did he?"

"Yeah. But I don't need all this checking. I'm not some sort of delicate flower. It was just a brunch."

"Yeah, but it's an awkward situation, and it puts you in a difficult position." Carter wasn't smiling. He looked subdued. "I never should have asked you to do this."

She reached over and rubbed his back. "It's fine, Carter. I wanted to help. It's really no problem. And Lincoln isn't as bad as I thought."

Her words didn't relax Carter as she'd hoped they would. In fact, his frown deepened. "I'm glad you're getting along. I heard y'all joking in here. Just..."

"Just what?"

"Just be careful."

"With what?"

"With Lincoln. He's... he's good at making people like him. He's not good at following through." His eyes scanned her face with obvious concern. "Just be careful."

"I'm always careful, Carter. I'm not going to do something stupid like get a crush on him. Do you really think I'm that stupid?"

"No. Of course not. I never thought that for even a moment. But even if you try to be his friend. He might... disappoint you. I know from experience. It hurts."

She leaned over to give him a one-armed hug. "I know he's hurt you before. I don't blame you for not trusting him right away. But I really do think he's trying. He's been... pretty good with me."

"Good. I'm glad. I hope... I hope he'll keep it up." He took a shaky breath. "Just don't trust him. Not completely. That never turns out well."

"Okay." She swallowed hard, her good mood from her conversation with Lincoln earlier sinking into an uncomfortable heaviness. "I'll be careful. I promise."

He brushed a light kiss on her cheek and stood up. "Good. Thank you. I'll let you rest."

She watched him leave the room, and then she stretched out on the bed again, feeling not quite as good as she had when Lincoln left.

4

———

A week later, late on a Friday afternoon, Summer was sitting next to Lincoln at a conference table in the office of Hiram Graves, the attorney who'd managed her trust fund ever since her grandmother died when Summer was sixteen. He was a competent man in his sixties who'd always done his job and never made any attempt to get to know her even though he'd been appointed her legal guardian for a year and a half until she'd turned eighteen.

Summer had never blamed him for not being anything but professional with her. He wasn't her family. There was no reason for him to act like he was. She'd spent her childhood being lonely, and her grandmother's death hadn't changed her situation in any real way. She'd never expected to be adopted into someone else's family. She'd just needed someone who was legally responsible for her until she was officially an adult.

Hiram was scrupulous with the administration of the money her grandmother had left her, and she never doubted that he took good care of it. She didn't have to like him or enjoy her meetings with him.

She'd gotten off work a few hours early, so she was dressed in her skirt, tall boots, and vintage velvet jacket. The heat in the suite was set too high, and it was stuffy in the room.

Lincoln wore jeans and a long-sleeved crewneck. Typically inappropriate for the occasion.

They'd been there for more than an hour already, and Summer was getting bored and restless from the way Hiram was reviewing every single point of the paperwork they were signing.

She already knew all those details. She'd already made her decision.

She didn't need to sit through the whole thing again and suffer through Hiram's looks of condescending disapproval.

Lincoln hadn't said much, but she could sense he was annoyed too. He felt tense beside her—a sure sign something was bothering him. He slanted a sideways look at her, catching her watching him. His thick eyebrows arched with a wordless question.

She gave her head a slight shake, assuming he'd understand the gesture as saying nothing was wrong and he shouldn't pursue the topic or interrupt Hiram's monotonous droning.

He did understand, and Hiram droned on undisturbed.

It was another twenty minutes before Hiram got to the final page. Summer reached for the expensive fountain pen that he'd set in front of her. As soon as she signed, this meeting would be over.

Instead of sliding her the page, Hiram met her eyes. "I believe this is a mistake."

She sighed. "I know that. You've told me more than once now. But this is my decision. Lincoln is my husband, so his family business is my family business as well. The terms of the trust allow me to use my money as I want in this situation."

"When your grandmother set out those terms, she assumed you wouldn't marry a man for no other reason than to throw your money away."

She'd never told Hiram the real reason she'd married Lincoln, but he wasn't a fool. The quick marriage followed immediately by the large investment in Wilson Hotels told a clear story. But suspicions were different from knowing for sure, and he couldn't do anything to block the investment unless he knew for sure that the marriage was a scam.

She gave him a cool glare. "I'm not throwing my money away. I'm investing in a business I believe in."

Hiram shook his balding head. "Your belief in it is based on personal affection and not on facts or numbers. Wilson Hotels has a history of being a bad investment that eats up every—"

"Enough," Lincoln broke in curtly. His voice was sharp but not loud.

Both Hiram and Summer turned to him in surprise.

Lincoln continued, "She's made her decision. She isn't a child. She's a mature, intelligent woman who has decided what she wants to do with her own money. You've voiced your concerns. Your job is done. The decision is Summer's, so allow her to make it."

Hiram curled up his lip—obviously unused to being

talked to that way—but he slid the final page over to Summer so she could sign and date it.

She felt weirdly fluttery as she did so. Her hair fell forward as she leaned over the table, and when she'd signed, she peeked through it over at Lincoln.

He wasn't looking at her. He was staring at an empty spot on the table.

She'd been on her own since she was sixteen, and she'd felt alone for long before that. She'd had to make her way through the world by herself. She'd had to face problems on her own and fight all her own battles.

She wasn't used to someone taking up for her the way Lincoln just had.

Obviously the marriage wasn't real, but it was kind of nice. To have a husband who stuck up for her. To have someone who was on her side.

Hiram said a few more things after she'd signed. She wasn't really listening. And a few minutes later she and Lincoln were leaving the office.

She kept shooting him little looks, wondering what he was thinking. He was uncharacteristically quiet as they walked through the reception area outside Hiram's office and into the main hallway of the law firm.

"Why do you keep peering at me?" Lincoln murmured, his eyes focused straight ahead.

She had no idea how he'd known she was watching him. "No reason." She felt her cheeks flushing slightly, although she didn't know why she would be embarrassed. "Just... thanks."

He stopped and turned to face her. "For what?"

"For that. Back there. For taking my side." She dropped

NOELLE ADAMS

her eyes but raised them again because she wanted to see his expression. "I'm not used to it."

He was frowning thoughtfully. "Not used to what?"

"I'm not used to not facing everything alone." She gulped, hardly believing she'd said something so vulnerable.

For just a moment she thought her words had affected him. His features twisted just slightly, like he was processing some sort of emotion. But then his mouth turned up in a little smile. "The man is a patronizing asshole, and I wanted him to shut up. It was way too hot in that room."

Ridiculously, she was disappointed in the way he'd turned her gratitude into an ironic joke. "Still."

He nodded, his smile fading into something else. "He was definitely being an ass, but he's right, you know."

"Right about what?"

"About your making a mistake."

She took an awkward step backward, wanting to put a little space between them. He always stood way too close. "I'm not making a mistake."

"Yes, you are. And deep down, you have to know it." He moved forward as she moved back until she was pinned against a wall, blocked by the position of his body. "Admit it."

She was tempted to push him away, but that would feel like a defeat. She tightened her jaw and glared up at him, her earlier fluttering gratitude transforming into indignation in an instant. "I'm not going to admit anything of the kind. I've thought everything through. I know what I'm doing."

"But you're not doing it because you believe in the future of Wilson fucking Hotels. You're doing it because you love Carter." He'd grown angry just as quickly as she had. His

70

voice was soft and rough, and his body was shuddering with pent-up feelings.

"What's wrong with that? Carter is as close to family as I've ever had. You do things for family that you wouldn't do for strangers. It's not wrong, and it's not unnatural. I have the money. It's only a very small amount—"

"It's millions of dollars. It's not a small amount."

"It's a small amount compared to the amount I have. I've got this huge pile of money. It was given to me. I did nothing to earn it. Why shouldn't I use a little of it to help someone I love? Tell me, Lincoln. Why shouldn't I?"

"You can do anything you want." His skin was damp with a faint sheen of perspiration. She didn't know if it was from the heat of the office or the intensity of whatever he was feeling. "Exactly as I told Graves. But you're throwing your money away. You know that, right? You're throwing it away." He planted a hand on the wall next to her shoulder and tilted his head down toward hers.

Lincoln was standing only a few inches from her. She could reach out and touch him. She wanted to so much that she had to clench her fingers at her sides. "You say that because you assume I'm expecting to get the money back. I'm not. It's not an investment for me. It's a gift. It's a *gift*, Lincoln. Carter needs it, and I have it to give him. You don't expect to get a gift back."

He was breathing heavily. She could hear the raspy rhythm of it. See his chest rise and fall.

"Why does it make you so angry?" Summer demanded. "Why do you care what I do with my money? Why does it have anything to do with you?"

"Maybe I'm tired of seeing it."

"Seeing what?"

"Seeing you throwing your heart away to Carter when he's never—*never*—going to want it the way he should. He's *never* going to recognize what it's worth." His eyes were on fire, flashing with a passionate resentment that made her breathless.

Her mouth was bone dry. She licked her lips and swallowed. "That's not... that's not what's happening."

"Isn't it? Hasn't it been happening since high school?"

"No. I mean, maybe when I was younger, I had some... You were right about prom. About how I felt back then. But not now. That's not why I'm doing this now."

Something was changing on his face, but she couldn't recognize what the difference was. He scanned her face urgently. "Then why are you?"

She felt exposed. Stripped bare. Like he could see into the heart of her in a way no one else ever had.

It terrified her.

She didn't know this man very well. He wasn't a stranger, but he also wasn't a friend. And Carter was right. He couldn't necessarily be trusted.

Not with the deepest parts of her.

She licked her lips again. "I don't... know."

He leaned even closer. She could feel his breath on her flushed skin. "Yes, you do know. Tell me."

Normally, this kind of intensity would make her so uncomfortable she'd retreat. She'd give in just to have the confrontation over. But she wasn't going to give in to Lincoln. "No. I'm not going to tell you. And you can't intimidate me into it."

"I'm not trying to intimidate—"

"Look at yourself!" she interrupted sharply. "Look at how you're standing. You've got me trapped against this wall. And you're really going to claim you're not trying to intimidate me?"

He blinked. Then looked down at himself. At her. At his hand braced on the wall. He dropped it suddenly and stepped back. "I wasn't doing that on purpose."

"I know you weren't. You're used to people giving in to you. You're used to women swooning at your feet because you offer them nothing but your hotness. And you find it frustrating that I won't."

He narrowed his eyes. "I'm not expecting you to swoon at my feet."

"Aren't you? Isn't that why you're always so annoyed with me?"

"No. It's not. And you should know me better than that by now."

"I know you plenty well. And you're fooling yourself if you don't realize how easily you can normally get people to do what you want them to do. And how impatient you get when they won't."

"My impatience with you has nothing to do with not making you do what I want you to do."

"You're lying."

"No." He planted his hand on the wall again. "I'm not."

They glared at each other until Summer's anger transformed into a rush of need and desire that nearly buckled her knees. She wanted to touch him. Kiss him. Run her hands all over his big, tense body.

It was literally painful to hold herself back from doing so.

She had no idea what she would have done or said—or

what Lincoln would have done or said—had she not become conscious of another presence in the hallway.

She turned her head and saw Carter standing a few feet away. He was frozen with a look of confused disbelief. And something else. Something deep and aching. His eyes shifted back and forth between her and Lincoln.

Suddenly terrified and more self-conscious than she would have been had Carter caught them with Lincoln's hand down her pants, Summer pushed Lincoln backward. Not hard but firmly enough to move his body.

"Hey, Carter," she said, forcing a casual cheer she wasn't feeling. "I didn't know you were coming by."

Carter blinked a few times before meeting her eyes. "I was just stopping by to check on things." He glanced over toward Lincoln, who was standing tense and silent. "Everything okay?"

"Yeah. Lincoln and I were just having a... disagreement. But it's no big deal."

It felt like a big deal, but she didn't know why.

"Okay," Carter said slowly. "You want to get some coffee or something?"

"Sure," Summer said with a smile that she hoped was more natural. "That sounds good."

Both she and Carter turned to look at Lincoln.

His face was dead sober as he looked between Summer and his brother. "I don't know if I was part of that invitation, but I've got stuff to do. I'll see you guys later."

Without another word and without glancing again at her, he made his way down the hall toward the elevator.

Summer's stomach twisted. She felt heavy. Guilty. Confused.

And she couldn't help but resent Lincoln for making her feel that way.

Carter still looked kind of upset, even after his brother had left. Summer went over to take his arm. "It's fine, Carter. It was nothing."

"It didn't look like nothing. It looked like you..." Carter took a shaky breath.

"It looked like what?"

"It looked... intimate."

She gasped. "It wasn't intimate! There's nothing intimate between Lincoln and me."

"Are you sure?"

"We were fighting. We weren't kissing or anything."

"I don't know why, but it looked like you were doing both. At the same time."

"We weren't!" Her voice cracked. This whole thing was terrible, and she had no idea how to make it better. "I'm not that close to Lincoln. We're just married so we can get access to my trust fund. You know that. It's almost over. We can get divorced in another month or so. Then I won't have to worry about Lincoln ever again."

Despite her words, the idea of being done with Lincoln made her heart sink more than ever.

Carter exhaled deeply and rubbed his face. "I never should have done this to you."

"You didn't do anything to me."

"Yes, I did. I got you into this mess. And if you end up getting hurt, it's all on me."

"It's not on you, and I'm not going to get hurt. I'm not a silly girl who falls for a hot body, pretty eyes, and a cocky attitude. You know I'm not."

"I know you're not. That's not what I'm worried about."

"Then what?"

He bit his lower lip and then quickly released it. "I don't even know. But I really screwed up. I screwed up bad. Everything that happens now is all my fault."

She tried to argue some more since he was wrong. She knew he was wrong. But he was walking toward the elevator, so she didn't get the chance.

THAT EVENING, Summer was getting ready for bed at around ten. It was early, but she was exhausted and hadn't felt like going out. So she took a long bath and changed into a pretty white camisole and lavender pajama pants.

She was brushing her hair when there was a knock on the door.

With a surprised jerk, she turned toward the main door of the room before she realized the knock hadn't come from there.

It had come from the private door that connected her room to Lincoln's.

Confused and strangely nervous, she walked over. "Yes?"

"Can you open the door, Summer?" Lincoln's voice was slightly muffled by the barrier between them.

"Why?"

"For God's sake, I'm not planning to have my wicked way with you. I want to talk for a minute."

Despite the faint annoyance in his tone, she hesitated. Her hand was slightly shaky as she reached for the lock.

When she swung the door open, Lincoln was standing

across the threshold. He wore the same thing he'd been wearing earlier in the day, but his hair was more rumpled and his eyelids were heavy.

"Why aren't you at work?"

"I have the week off." His eyes ran up and down her body from her loose hair to the hairbrush in her hand to her bare feet. His eyes lingered just a little longer on her breasts through the thin fabric of her top.

"Why?"

"Because I have vacation time, and I have to use it sometime. Can we talk for a minute?"

"I thought we were talking now."

He rolled his eyes, and she relented, stepping out of the way so he could come into her bedroom.

She stayed standing where she was rather than getting anywhere close to the bed. She found him way too attractive. She thought about sex far too much when he was around. She wasn't going to risk it.

"Are we all right?" Lincoln asked.

"With what?"

"With earlier. Our argument or whatever it was. Are we all right?"

She nodded. "Yes. We're all right. You're an exasperating person, but I'm used to that by now. I'm not still mad or anything."

"Good. Then have you talked to Carter this evening?"

Her eyes widened. "Tonight? No. Not since we had coffee this afternoon. I didn't see him, so I figured he was out on a date or something."

"He's not. He's home."

"Really? Where is he?"

"He's in the library with the door closed. He's drinking. A lot."

Summer's eyes grew even rounder. "What? Carter doesn't drink a lot. I don't think I've ever seen him drunk before."

"That's because he doesn't let you see it. But he does drink occasionally. When he's really upset about something." Lincoln's face was as close to worried as she'd ever seen it. "He's upset about something now."

"He was kind of upset earlier because he was feeling guilty. He thinks he pressured me into this marriage."

"He did pressure you into this marriage."

"Lincoln, stop it with that. It's not helping anything. Anyway, he was a little upset earlier, but I talked him out of it."

"I don't think you did. He's still upset. He's drinking a lot."

Summer looked toward the main door of her room as if Carter might be lurking in the hallway. "Are you sure? Carter doesn't do that."

"Summer, listen to me." Lincoln reached over and put a hand on her shoulder, turning her back around to face him. "Carter *does* do that. Not much, but occasionally. He's never let you see him do it because he likes for you to think he's a perfect hero. He likes you to think he's a saint."

"I don't think—"

"He's not a saint, Summer. He's a much better man than me, but he's also a regular human being who messes up sometimes and doesn't always handle it well. He's wallowing in guilt right now, and he's trying to drink himself into a stupor."

His sober tone and expression convinced her. With a rush of urgency, she hurried over to grab a soft bathrobe from the back of the bathroom door. "And you just left him there alone?"

"He didn't want me there. I was making it worse. He needs you, so I came to get you."

Summer quickly tied the sash of her robe and slid on a pair of slippers. "Thanks for telling me. I'll talk to him."

She was on her way out the door when Lincoln grabbed her arm. "Hey, wait a minute."

Pausing, she gazed up at his handsome face. "What?"

Lincoln held her gaze without wavering. "Carter might not be a sinner like me, but he's not a saint. Don't expect him to be one. It makes it harder for him when he can't live up."

Summer let the words process. Then she nodded. Pulled out of his grip. And walked away from him.

When she reached the library, the door was closed. It wasn't a private room of the house, but it was unusual for the door to be closed, so she knocked a few times before she opened it.

"Go away, Lincoln!" Carter's voice was muffled and slightly slurred. Not like him at all.

She stepped into the room and found her friend slumped in a leather armchair near the large marble fireplace. He had the gas log turned on—blazing far too high for the room. It felt like she was walking into an oven. "It's not Lincoln."

There was a delay before his jerk of surprise. Clearly his mind wasn't working as quickly as usual. He held a mostly empty glass of what looked and smelled like bourbon. "Go away, Summer."

"I don't want to go away. What are you doing in here?" She came over to sit in the leather chair opposite his. She was already sweating from the heat of the fireplace.

"What does it look like?" He finished off the liquor in his glass and then leaned over to grab a bottle from a side table to pour himself another.

Definitely bourbon.

"This is ridiculous, Carter. How much of that have you drunk?"

He shrugged.

"This isn't like you."

His brown eyes were hazy and his lids heavy, but he managed to give her a sideways glare that was speakingly annoyed.

She remembered what Lincoln had said and went on. "Okay. Maybe it is. Occasionally. But there's no reason for you to drink yourself silly. You didn't do anything wrong."

He huffed. And kept huffing. She supposed he was laughing, but it wasn't like any laughter she'd heard from him before.

"Carter, please." She leaned over and reached out to squeeze his knee. "I'm fine. I'm perfectly happy. I'm not hurt in any way by this marriage. You don't have to feel guilty."

"I don't feel guilty," he mumbled, staring at the fire rather than at her. "I feel..."

"You feel what?"

"I feel..." He trailed off again. Didn't finish the thought. Just took another big swallow of bourbon.

"Carter—"

"Summer, if you're going to sit in here with me when I've

asked you not to, the least you can do is not yammer the whole time."

A pang of pain and defensiveness slashed through her chest at the words—far ruder than Carter's normal kind nature—but she didn't let herself react with words. No good would come with arguing with him right now. He was obviously hurting. If she was going to help him, she couldn't let him feel even worse.

"Okay," she said softly. "Then the least you can do is pour me a glass of that."

He glanced at the bottle, as if the fact that he was still holding it surprised him. Then he shrugged and stretched the full length of his body to reach a clean glass from the bar. He poured her a drink and handed it to her.

She took a small sip. The taste was good. Warm. Filling. But stronger than she preferred her drinks to be.

But she wasn't going to leave Carter here all by himself.

She sat with him for almost an hour. It took nearly the whole time for her to finish her glass. Carter drunk his down and poured himself another, but after that he sat holding his empty glass, staring at the fake fire.

She didn't know if her presence was helping anything, but he'd asked her not to talk, so she didn't.

"Go to bed, Summer," Carter finally muttered. He still wasn't looking at her.

"I don't want to. Not until you do."

"I'm going to bed soon."

"Are you?"

"Yeah." He didn't move.

"Carter—"

"Summer, don't."

She straightened, trying not to respond emotionally. But it hurt. A lot. Carter never treated her like this, and she didn't understand what had gotten into him now.

Lincoln said this wasn't the first time he'd broken down like this, but she'd never seen it happen before. She didn't like it. She wanted it to be over. She wanted to fix it but had no idea how to do so.

"Summer, I know you want to help." Carter finally turned to meet her gaze with eyes that looked pained, bleary. "But there's nothing you can do right now. So can you please back off a little? I need some space."

"But why do you need space from *me*?"

"It's not just you. It's everyone. I'm asking you. If you're my friend, you'll give me some space for a few days."

She gulped. Nodded. Carefully set her glass down before she rose to her feet. "Okay. But I love you, Carter. And I know you love me too. You've never hurt me. So please don't feel bad on my account."

He stared at her blankly. She wasn't even sure if her words had registered. With nothing else to do, she left the room, her eyes burning as she returned to her bedroom.

IT WAS LATE—WELL past midnight—when she brushed her teeth, went to the bathroom, and climbed into bed. But she wasn't sleepy. There was no way she could sleep. So she turned on the television and flipped around until she found an old sitcom she could tolerate.

She'd been watching it blindly for about ten minutes when there was a knock on the door.

Not her main door but the one that connected to Lincoln's room.

"It's still open," she called out.

Lincoln opened the door, letting in a wash of light from his room. His body was silhouetted against it for a moment— a lean, dark, faceless figure—until he took several steps toward her bed.

She could see him better now. He was dressed for bed in pajama pants and nothing else. He stood above her, gazing down at her face.

"Is he okay?" he asked softly.

She swallowed hard. "I don't know. I don't think so. He wouldn't talk to me."

"Give him time."

"That's what he said, but it's hard. He's hurting, and I want to help him."

"I'm not sure there's anything you can do for him right now."

"You said he's done this before?"

"Yeah. Several times I can remember."

"I've never seen him like this before."

"Because he's never let you. I told you before. He wants you to only ever see him be strong. He'll keep weakness from you if he possibly can. Let him sulk for a day or two. He'll snap out of it. He always does."

"You're sure?" She adjusted the covers up over her shoulders since Lincoln's eyes kept slipping down to her chest. Her camisole wasn't all that thick, and her nipples were probably visible through the fabric.

He met her eyes again. "Yes, I'm sure."

"Okay." She sighed and stretched out, trying to relax.

83

Tomorrow was Saturday, so she didn't have work in the morning, but she'd made brunch and shopping plans with a couple of her friends, so she couldn't sleep until noon.

She'd expected Lincoln to leave after confirming the condition of his brother, but he didn't. He stood quietly, looking at her in the light and shadow of the room.

"What?" she finally demanded.

"Are *you* okay?"

With a weird pressure in her throat, she admitted, "I... don't know."

"It's hard when an idol falls, isn't it?"

"Carter wasn't an idol to me."

"Wasn't he?"

"No. I mean, yes, I had some silly daydreams about him. In the past. Not now. But I'm not upset right now because he's not a flawless hero."

"Then what are you upset about?" It sounded like he really wanted to know.

"I don't know. I'm worried about Carter. I don't like to see him in pain. And... and..."

"And what?"

"And I guess I'm kind of sad." She licked her lips and tried to think through the tumble of emotion inside her. "It feels like I'm... I'm leaving something behind. And it makes me sad."

Lincoln took a step closer to the bed. "What are you leaving behind?"

"I don't know." It was a lie. She knew exactly what she was moving beyond. All her old hopes and dreams and feelings for Carter. They'd been important to her. Special. They'd

84

given her something to hope for when she'd had nothing else.

But they'd died completely now, leaving her with a strange sort of grief.

"Yes, you do. Tell me. What are you leaving behind, Summer?" Lincoln was urgent. Inappropriately urgent for the nature of their conversation.

She shrugged. She knew Lincoln now. She understood him. She even liked him most of the time. But Carter had been right. It would be dangerous to trust him.

So she had to keep her most intimate thoughts to herself, no matter how tempted she was to share.

"Summer—"

"Stop pushing, Lincoln. It's not your business what I'm feeling right now."

"But I want to know."

"Have you found in life that you always get what you want?"

"No." He gave a soft huff of dry amusement. "Almost never."

"So why would you assume you'd get what you want right now?"

His tense expression softened into a smile. "Why is it that you're this stubborn and determined only with me?"

"I'm not like this only with you."

"Aren't you? From my observation, you're sweet and accommodating with everyone else. We could ask any of our mutual acquaintances, and they'd all testify to that fact. So why don't I get any of your sweetness?"

To her dismay, she felt herself blushing and flutters awakened in her heart. Hopefully he wouldn't be able to see her reaction because of the darkness of the room. "Because you don't deserve it. You be sweet to me, and I'll be sweet to you."

As soon as she heard the words in the air, she wished she hadn't said them.

He took the final step toward the bed. He was close enough to touch now. He murmured thickly, "I can be as sweet as you want. Just say the word."

Her whole body went hot. A throb of arousal pulsed between her legs. It took all the willpower she possessed to keep her voice even as she said, "Get out of here, Lincoln."

With an almost wicked smile, he turned toward the connecting door between their rooms. "You can't run forever, Summer."

"I'm not running. I'm going to sleep. Now get out of here."

"Your wish is my..." He was laughing as he walked out of the room.

Summer didn't see Carter all day on Saturday. Or Sunday. Or Monday.

She was really starting to worry.

On Sunday afternoon, she sent him a casual text message. Just checking in. There was no answer, so she tried again on Monday morning. Then again on Monday afternoon. She tried calling after dinner on Monday, but the call just went to voice mail.

Lincoln had said Carter would bounce back in a day or two, but it had been three days now and nothing. Carter had just disappeared.

She tried once more before she got into bed on Monday

night, but there was no answer again. She wanted to talk to Lincoln—since he was the only thing that had made her feel better all weekend—but he'd gone out with friends that evening.

So instead she turned on the television and pulled up Netflix, searching for a few minutes until she found a show she liked and hadn't watched for a while.

She'd gotten through about thirty minutes of an episode when there was a knock on the connecting door. "It's open!" she called with a surge of relief and excitement. She hadn't locked the door since Lincoln had come in to tell her about Carter on Friday evening.

Lincoln opened the door and came in. He wore dark jeans, a black T-shirt, and a black leather jacket. He smelled like whiskey and night air. "You in bed already?"

"It's eleven. It's not that early. I have to go to work tomorrow morning. Not all of us are on a week's vacation."

Lincoln gave her a quirk of a smile as he walked over to the opposite side of the bed. He toed off his shoes, dropped his jacket on the floor, and flopped down on top of the covers beside her.

She frowned at him. "Just go ahead and make yourself comfortable."

"I am. What are we watching?"

"We aren't watching anything. I was watching in the privacy of my room until you came barging in uninvited."

"You said it was open." He grinned at her—ridiculously appealing—before he turned toward the television. "Zombies? Really?"

"Why are you surprised? The early seasons were really good."

"I don't know. I just expected you to be absorbed in some schmaltzy animated Disney movie."

She made a choked sound. "Why would you think that?"

"Don't you like that kind of thing?" He turned toward her again, his eyes laughing, fond, uncharacteristically soft.

She scowled at him, trying to stifle the swell of pleasure and affection. "Occasionally. But not all the time. Sometimes I like to watch regular people trying to survive a zombie apocalypse."

He chuckled and turned toward the television. They watched in silence until the episode was over.

She turned on her side so she was facing Lincoln. "Have you talked to Carter?"

He shifted to face her too. "Not since Friday."

"Me either. Have you heard from him at all? Seen him?"

"No." Lincoln frowned. "You mean you haven't heard anything from him for three days?"

"Nothing. I'm getting worried. He hasn't been sleeping here. He won't answer his phone. He didn't go into the office today."

"Maybe he's staying with a friend."

"I've called all his friends. No one has heard from him. No one has seen him. He's just vanished off the face of the earth." She reached over and touched his forearm, which was resting on the bed between them. "Lincoln, I'm getting scared."

"I'm sure it's nothing to worry about." He brushed a loose strand of hair off her face. "Don't be scared. He does this. He always snaps back. Maybe he's..." He trailed off with a thoughtful frown.

"He disappears completely? For more than three days? Has he done this before, Lincoln?"

"Not for so long. And he usually just hides away at home. But I'm sure he's okay. Please don't be scared." He acted like he was brushing her hair back again, but there wasn't any hair on her face. He was just brushing his fingers lightly against her cheek, and it felt so good it made her shudder.

But she was too worried about Carter to indulge that kind of feeling right now. "I'm trying not to be."

"I'll see what I can find out." Lincoln rolled off the bed and stood up, reaching down to grab his jacket and shoes from the floor.

Her chest relaxed. She smiled up at him in relieved gratitude. "Thank you."

He stared at her for a moment. She couldn't read the expression in his eyes. Then he gave his head a quick shake and he smiled. "Don't worry. I'm sure your prince is off grooming his white steed somewhere. But I'll see if I can track him down."

"Thanks, Lincoln. Let me know if you find anything."

"I will." He went into his bedroom and closed the door, leaving her with nothing but the light of the television.

SUMMER WAS STILL WIDE-AWAKE an hour later when there was another knock on the door.

"Come in!" Her voice cracked slightly on the second word.

Lincoln swung the door open and stood in the doorway. "I found him."

She sat up in bed, the covers falling down to her waist. She was wearing a cute knit gown in a dusty pink. "You found him?"

"Yeah. He's not being very stealthy. He's putting every-thing on his credit card. He's in Atlantic City."

"Atlantic City! What is he doing there?"

"Well, from the credit card purchases, he's spending a ridiculous amount of money at bars and casinos."

"Oh no." She covered her mouth with one hand. "Lincoln—"

"I know. I know."

"This is not normal. He might really be in trouble, Lincoln."

"I *know*." His voice was slightly rough. He combed his fingers through his messy hair.

"What are we going to do? We have to do something. We have to help him."

"Yeah." Lincoln met her eyes across the distance and the bluish light of the television. "You want to go get him? Bring him home?"

"Yes. Yes, please!"

"There's a flight from Charlotte at seven in the morning. You want me to get us tickets?"

"Yes. Thank you." She got out of bed and hurried over to where he was standing. She reached out and grabbed for one of his arms. "Thank you, Lincoln."

He gave a half shrug, looking slightly uncomfortable. "He's my brother. And he's obviously taken a tumble off his noble white steed. We'll find him. We'll haul him back up into the saddle where he belongs."

Summer was so relieved and gratified and filled with fond feelings that she wrapped her arms around him, squeezing his lean, hard body in a hug.

Lincoln didn't react immediately. He stood stiffly for so

long she was about to draw back. But then his arms went around her too. He tightened them for a few seconds before he released her.

She pulled back, flushed and smiling. "I'll be ready first thing tomorrow. I'll take a couple of days off work. Thank you for finding him."

"You're welcome." He was smiling too, but there was something else smoldering in his eyes. "But just a word of advice. That nightgown does nothing to hide your body. So unless you want to take me up on my offer of a good time, then you might put a robe on before you hug me again."

She gasped and glanced down at herself. Crossed her arms on her chest.

Lincoln chuckled. "That's what I thought. Be ready by the crack of dawn tomorrow. We'll need to get an early start."

She didn't have time to say anything else before he was leaving and closing the door behind him.

Summer stared at the closed door for a long time. She didn't lock it before she finally crawled back into bed.

5

THE FOLLOWING MORNING, SUMMER WOKE FROM A LIGHT SLEEP and couldn't seem to open her eyes.

She was awake. She knew she was. She could think conscious thoughts and assess her physical condition. But her head and body and eyelids were all heavy. Too heavy to sit up straight or open her eyes.

She wasn't uncomfortable. She was leaning over, resting on something warm and firm. There was soft fabric beneath her cheek. A pleasant weight wrapped around the back of her shoulders. And she was surrounded by the most delicious smell. Warm and familiar. Both natural and expensive. Slightly spicy but only on the surface. There was an underlying note that was... human.

Lincoln.

She was surrounded by the smell of Lincoln.

Shifting slightly, she rubbed her cheek against the fabric. It felt so nice. So did the firmness of the substance beneath it. It was hard. Heat was coming from it. But it wasn't unyielding.

It moved occasionally. And when she was very still, she could feel a pulsing from inside it.

A heartbeat.

Lincoln's heart.

She gasped and raised her head, tilting it up to see Lincoln's face a couple of inches from hers. For a moment she had no idea where she was. The only thing she was conscious of was those unnaturally vivid green eyes. The expression in them. Filled with a softness that mesmerized her.

Without thinking, she stretched toward him, desperately needing to meet the feeling in his gaze, to bury herself in it.

The sound of coughing from somewhere behind her finally brought her to her senses. She pulled back. Straightened up. Stretched her back and rubbed her face.

They were in the first-class cabin of an airplane heading to Atlantic City. She'd obviously fallen asleep and leaned over on top of him without realizing it. He must have raised the armrest between them and wrapped an arm around her to hold her in place.

And she'd almost kissed him as she woke up.

She risked a glance over to him and saw he was watching her with familiar laughter on his face. A teasing kind of laughter.

She scowled at him. "I was asleep."

"I know that. For almost half an hour."

"I didn't mean to lay all over you."

"Obviously. But I didn't mind."

"If you hadn't raised the armrest, I wouldn't have been so much on top of you."

He twitched his eyebrows. "That's why I raised it."

She was blushing. She couldn't help it. Plus one of her

cheeks was hotter than the other from the way it had been pressed against his shirt. She probably looked ridiculous.

Smoothing down her hair, she gave Lincoln another mild glare.

He laughed out loud, stretching his legs and lowering the armrest. "Anytime you need a pillow, I'll gladly oblige."

"Uh-huh."

"And anytime you need a blanket to keep you warm, I can be that too."

She rolled her eyes. He was obviously teasing, but she couldn't help but like the sound of it.

"And if you ever need a sex toy to give you some physical release, I can provide that too."

She gasped and jerked away. "Lincoln!"

"What? Too much?"

"Yes, it's too much. I wish you wouldn't do that."

"Do what?"

"Tease like that. In that way."

He leaned forward and murmured thickly, "In the sexy way?"

"Yes, in the sexy way." Her whole body was hot, but she managed to meet his eyes evenly. "It makes me uncomfortable."

"If it really makes you uncomfortable, then I'll stop. But tell me the truth. Are you uncomfortable because you don't want to hear those things from me? Or is it because you *do* want to hear them but don't want to admit that to yourself?"

She was shaking, and she didn't know why. Maybe because his expression was both hot and strangely sincere. Or maybe because she was suddenly so scared her hands had gone cold. She cleared her throat. "I'm uncomfortable because it doesn't seem appropriate. We don't have that kind of relationship. And you shouldn't say things you know embarrass me when you don't mean them."

He blinked a couple of times and stiffened his shoulders. "What?"

"What, what?"

"You think I don't mean them?"

"Well, yes. I mean no. Whatever the right answer is. I don't think you really mean them. You're teasing the way you always do. You're trying to get a rise out of me. It's what you've always done ever since I was seventeen and you sent me those flowers the day after prom to embarrass Carter and me."

"You think I don't want to take you to bed?" His voice was soft and slightly rough.

She licked her lips since they were suddenly dry. "No. I mean, I guess you wouldn't say no to sex if it was offered, especially since otherwise you're out of luck until we get divorced. But I don't think you're really into me. I'm not stupid, you know."

"Yes, you are." He'd taken off his seat belt and turned in his seat to face her.

"No, I'm not! I know teasing when I see it, and all you do —all you've ever done—is tease."

The laughter in his eyes had died. He reached over and cupped her cheek. "You're wrong."

She pulled her face away from his hand since the touch was sending tingles of pleasure all through her body. "You don't really think I'm silly enough to believe you're into me."

"If by *into* you mean I spend most of the time we're together imagining you in bed with me, fantasizing about kissing every inch of your body and making you come harder than you've ever come before, then yes. I'm definitely into you."

She gulped. Crossed her arms over her belly since it felt like she needed to hold herself together.

He raised a hand like he would touch her again but then dropped it onto the armrest. "Listen to me, Summer. This is the truth. I sound teasing because I'm trying not to be pushy or pressure you. You're stuck in a bad situation. You should never be married to me like this. But I mean what I say to you." He held her gaze. Deep and intense. Soul-shaking. "I mean everything."

"O...kay." She had to look away since otherwise she'd melt into a puddle right there in the airline seat. "I... I..."

"Yes?"

She caught herself just when she was on the verge of admitting she was dying to have sex with him too. "I don't think it's a good idea."

"What isn't a good idea?"

"Us. Having sex. It's... It would make things too complicated."

"It wouldn't have to. I know how to avoid strings. I've done it all my life."

"I know you have, but I haven't." She finally dared to look at him again and was relieved to see his typical relaxed amusement. "I'm sure sex would be... be..."

"Earth-shattering."

She couldn't help but snicker at his dry tone. "Fun. But I take sex seriously. I never do it unless there's more than fun between us. And our situation is weird enough without adding casual sex into the mix. So I think we better not."

"Understood."

She checked his expression but didn't see any disappointment or resentment. He looked as relaxed as normal, which was a relief.

And also a tiny bit of a letdown.

Pushing aside that feeling, since it was ridiculous and irrational, she wisely changed the subject. "So what are we going to do when we get there? It's going to be pretty early."

"Yeah. If Carter has really been living it up the way it looks from his credit card record, then he'll probably still be sleeping it off when we arrive. We'll head to the hotel he's been booked in for the past two nights, and I'll see if I can talk any of the staff into spilling which room he's in."

"They're not going to just give out that information."

"I can be pretty persuasive."

She snorted. "Let me guess. You're going to find a susceptible female and woo the information out of her."

"Woo isn't the word I'd use."

"Seduce." She shook her head. "You can be a real dick, you know."

"I know that. And if I ever forget, I always have you to remind me. But we've got to figure it out somehow. If that doesn't work, I'll call the hotel and ask to be connected to his room. If he picks up the phone, I'll let you convince him to come talk to us. He won't want to say no to you."

"Okay. I guess it's a plan. What if he doesn't want to come home with us?"

"We'll worry about that if it happens. We have to find the noble idiot first."

$\sim$

A FEW HOURS LATER, their rideshare dropped them off at the main entrance of a large hotel and casino. Summer usually arranged for hired cars to pick her up from airports, but Lincoln said rideshares were less hassle, and he was right.

It wasn't even noon, but there was already a lot of activity in the entryway and lobby.

Summer hated casino resorts like this. She hated all the fake glitz and all the noise and lights and distracting décor and all the unnatural fervor that shuddered in the manufactured air. As soon as she walked in, she shrank into herself, immediately wanting to walk back out.

"Y'okay?" Lincoln asked, turning to look down at her. He'd waved away the bell staff, so he was carrying his overnight bag on his shoulder and rolling her small suitcase behind him. He wore a slate-blue button-up shirt and black trousers and looked way too sexy for just getting off a plane.

"Yeah. Fine. Just don't like it here."

He put a hand on her back and moved her to an out-of-the-way corner with an upholstered bench. "Why don't you wait here with the stuff? I'll see if I can get us rooms."

"It's too early to check in."

"Maybe. But I doubt they're full on a Monday in late January. And I need to find someone to ask about Carter anyway. Just wait here where it's quiet."

She sniffed. "Don't think you're fooling me. You're not looking out for me. You just don't want me tagging along and cramping your style as you work your wooing magic."

He chuckled and tilted his head down to brush a very light kiss on her cheekbone. "Almost right. But I told you before. I don't woo."

She couldn't help but giggle. And try not to get too fluttery at his unexpected kiss. She wasn't going to make a big deal about it though. She sat on the bench as Lincoln set his bag beside her and rolled her case within her arm's reach.

She watched as he walked toward the front desk. There were a few people talking to the staff there, and she shook her head as she saw Lincoln make a beeline for a young, attractive woman who wasn't working with any of the guests.

There was no doubt about it. He'd get the information they needed. And probably end up getting them the best rooms in the hotel.

The man was way too hot. Way too charming. Way too used to getting his way. It made him genuinely dangerous.

She'd made the right decision about saying no to his offer of sex.

God help the poor fool who fell for Lincoln Wilson. She might as well try to take a leisurely swim in shark-infested waters. Nothing but danger and heartbreak lay in that direction.

Summer was over thirty now. She was too grown-up to make that kind of adolescent mistake.

FOURTEEN HOURS LATER, Summer got out of the shower and dried herself off with a thick white hotel towel.

She was exhausted and discouraged and on the verge of tears. But she'd already cried once today—by herself in a bathroom stall out of sheer frustration after endless hours of searching futilely for Carter—so she really didn't want to break down again.

She pulled on soft fleece pajama pants and a tank top.

Then stared at her face in the bathroom mirror. There were shadows under her eyes. She put on moisturizer, but it did nothing to improve her appearance. She pulled her hair out of the ponytail she'd worn in the shower and left it loose to sleep in. Brushing her teeth completed her nighttime routine, so she left the bathroom, turned out the lights and turned on the television, and then climbed into bed.

Lincoln had gotten them upgraded rooms that connected by a door between them. He'd easily gotten Carter's room number from the hotel staff, and when his brother failed to answer their knocks, he'd convinced a member of house-keeping to let them into the room.

Carter's stuff had been there, but he hadn't been.

They spent the rest of the day searching for him, but he'd stopped using his credit card, so they'd had to rely on asking people if they'd seen him and staking out his room.

They'd spent the past two hours in the hall near his room, waiting to see if he'd return. He hadn't. Summer had been willing to wait all night, but Lincoln had insisted they give up and go to bed. They could pound on his door first thing in the morning. Surely he'd be back there by then.

Summer had been hoping that she'd go to sleep quickly since she was so exhausted, but her mind was whirling, and she couldn't even close her eyes for very long.

She was almost relieved at the knock on the connecting door.

"It's unlocked," she called. She hadn't bothered to lock her side of the door after they'd had it open to plan their search earlier in the day.

Lincoln came into the room, wearing a pair of dark

pajama pants and nothing else. He stood and looked at her in bed. "Everything all right?"

"Yeah. Why wouldn't it be?"

"I don't know. I could just feel all these angsty vibes wafting their way under the crack in the door and invading the air of my room."

She huffed in tired amusement and pulled the covers up toward her shoulders. "I'm fine. Just kind of glum."

"Yeah." Lincoln walked around the bed to the other side. It didn't surprise her when he stretched out beside her, on top of the covers.

She turned on her side toward him. "I'm really worried about him."

"Yeah."

"Tell me the truth. This isn't normal. I know you said he's gone on binges before, but they haven't been like this. Have they?"

Lincoln's eyes were sober. He was lying on his back, but his head was turned toward her. "No. They haven't been like this."

"What do you think has gotten into him? I mean, what's prompted this?"

"He feels guilty about making you marry me."

"But that's not enough. I mean, I can understand him feeling bad. But I'm fine. I'm fine, and everyone can see it. I'm not unhappy. You've been decent to me. Obnoxious but decent. So why would he react so... so...?" She couldn't think of the right word.

Lincoln shook his head slowly. "It does seem like an extreme reaction. I don't know what's prompting it. There's something going on with him that we don't know about."

"But why don't we know about it? You're his brother, and I'm his best friend. There's no one in the world closer to him than we are. So why don't we know what's going on?" She was getting emotional, and her voice cracked in response.

Lincoln brushed one of her cheeks with his fingertips. "Because he doesn't want us to know."

"Why not? We love him. More than anyone. Why wouldn't he want us to know?"

"Maybe..."

"Maybe what?"

He drew back his hand and looked away from her. "I don't know. Just a random thought. I hope it's not right. Surely it's not..." His features twisted very briefly.

It scared her. "Lincoln? What is it? Tell me."

"It's nothing. I don't think it's right. He's never... never once..."

She reached out to grab any part of him she could reach. It happened to be his upper arm. Her fingers wrapped around the firm contour of his bicep. "He's never what? If you know, you have to tell me."

"I don't know. I promise. Just random thoughts that are probably figments of my angst-ridden imagination. I really think it's just a lifetime of holding himself to impossible standards. No one can live up to it. So he's finally just fallen off the deep end. He'll be okay. We'll bring him home. He's going to be all right, Summer. I promise."

She nodded, feeling better when he met her eyes again.

"We'll find him tomorrow. And we won't go home until he's coming with us."

She slid her hand up his neck until she was touching his bristly jaw. She loved the texture of it beneath her fingertips.

"Thank you, Lincoln."

His body tightened. "You're welcome."

She couldn't stop herself from touching him. She ran her fingers along the line of his jaw. Toward his mouth. She brushed his lips before she realized what she was doing.

She pulled back with a jerk, both terrified and embarrassed.

His mouth quirked up on one side. "Tell me the truth, Summer."

She swallowed and grew very still. "About what?"

He hesitated for several seconds. She held her breath through the silence. Then he reached down to grab the throw blanket she'd spread over her lower legs. "Is this your gaggy?"

She always took the throw blanket when she traveled. It was small and light and velvety soft and a lovely rich shade of chocolate brown. "No, it's not my gaggy!"

"Your blankie?"

"No!" She shot him an outraged look. "It's a throw blanket. I take it with me because sometimes I'm cold and I like to have something to cover up with that doesn't require me getting under the sheets in bed. It's not a blankie or a gaggy!"

He chuckled and spread the blanket out over him. "If you say so."

"I do say so. And you obviously see the benefit of it since you're using it right now."

"That's just because you'd get mad at me if I tried to get under the covers with you."

"I'd definitely get mad. Don't even think about it."

"I won't. That's why I'm using your blankie." He twitched his eyebrows.

She dissolved into giggles and got more comfortable in

bed. They lay in silence for a few minutes, both of them focused on the television.

Eventually she turned back toward him. "Thank you, Lincoln."

"For what?"

"For making me smile. For making me feel better. I know you did it on purpose."

He gave a little shrug and surprised her by looking slightly self-conscious. "Maybe it made me feel better too."

The following morning, Summer woke up groggy and confused. Even more confused when she turned her head and discovered Lincoln was sleeping in the bed beside her.

It took several seconds for her to orient herself to where she was and what was happening, but she relaxed as soon as she did.

Lincoln was asleep on his back, bare chested and covered with her soft brown throw. He'd obviously fallen asleep last night after they'd talked and evidently hadn't woken up and moved back to his own bed.

It didn't matter. He was on his own side and on top of the covers. Nothing embarrassing or unduly disturbing had happened. And it was kind of nice to see him sleeping. He looked different. Softer. More vulnerable. Without the sharp edges of his personality, the amused gleam of his eyes, and the clever irony of his expression.

He had really thick, dark eyelashes. Inappropriately so.

"The force of your stare is disturbing my slumbers."

She giggled at his dry, mumbled comment. "Hey, you're

the one who couldn't manage to get to his own bed last night."

"Yeah." He opened his eyes and rolled over to face her. "Sorry about that. Not sure why I collapsed like that."

"Doesn't matter. Except you stole my blanket all night after you derided it so mockingly."

"Well, I figured you'd prefer it to my sharing your sheet."

"You're definitely not invited under my sheets."

They smiled at each other until Summer remembered she'd just woken up. Her hair was probably a mess. Her cheeks and neck were likely to be unattractively flushed. And one strap of her tank top was slipping down her shoulder.

She straightened it and turned onto her back, staring up at the ceiling.

"What's the matter?" Lincoln reached over to turn her head back to face him.

"Nothing."

"Why do you insist on lying to me when you're probably the worst liar in the world?"

"I am not a bad liar!"

"Yes, you are. You're way too earnest to be a good liar. Lying takes emotional distance, and you're really bad at that."

She scowled at him. "I am not earnest!"

He was laughing outright now, his eyes warm and soft. Almost tender.

She would have loved the look of him had she not been so unsettled by his assessment of her. "Stop laughing. You're wrong. I'm not that earnest."

He scooted closer to her, raising himself up so he was gazing down at her. "Look at you, Summer. You respond to my teasing with an earnest declaration about how you're not earnest."

"I did not—" She broke off because he was infuriatingly right.

He stroked one of her cheeks with the pad of his thumb. "Earnest isn't an insult, baby."

"It is when you laugh at me about it. And calling me baby isn't going to make up for it."

"I'm not trying to make up for it. I love that you're earnest. That you take things seriously. That you take *me* seriously."

She blinked, her heart starting to flutter at his feather-light caress and the look in his eyes. "Why wouldn't I take you seriously?"

"Most people don't."

"That's because you don't want people to take you seriously. If all you do is tease and make sarcastic comments and laugh at people with your eyes, then they're not going to look beyond the surface."

"So why do you?"

She wasn't sure if her racing heart and pulsing blood was from fear or excitement, but it felt like the world had stopped —time had stopped—freezing around this one moment. Lincoln. And her. In bed. Inches apart. Gazing at each other. "I... I don't know. Because I think there's more to you than you want to show to the world. Because I don't think you're as bad as you pretend to be."

"Yeah?" His voice was no more than a rasp.

"Yeah."

He leaned down, and she was sure he would kiss her. She wanted him to. She'd never wanted anything more.

But his mouth moved toward her ear instead of her lips.

And he whispered, "That's because you're earnest."

The almost taunting tone was like a blow to her shuddering excitement. But it wasn't all bad. Part of her was intensely relieved he'd moved them past that terrifying moment. She gave an exaggerated gasp and pushed him away. "Asshole."

"Definitely." He winked at her as he sat up and got up from the bed, pulling up his pajama pants as he did since they'd slid down way too far. "And don't you forget it."

Her eyes ran up and down the beautifully toned lines of his body. There was no way not to leer a little at the gorgeousness of his half-naked form. But she was thinking about his last comment as he headed for his own room.

Maybe it had just been his normal banter, but it felt like there was something significant in the words.

She thought about them for a long time.

AFTER THEY GOT DRESSED and had breakfast, they staked out Carter's hotel room for a couple of hours until the housekeepers got nervous and asked them to leave.

So they moved their vigil to the lobby right where the elevators opened, so they could catch Carter as soon as he came downstairs.

They waited for hours, taking turns going to the bathroom, stretching their legs, or buying snacks for them to eat. Finally Lincoln got impatient and played up to an assistant manager, making up a sob story about his brother and convincing her to let him into his room.

Sadly, that led to the discovery that Carter had never

returned last night, which meant several hours of their day had been wasted.

Lincoln returned to the sofa in the lobby where she'd been sitting with this depressing news. He collapsed beside her with a groan that embodied exactly the way she felt herself.

"Can we check to see if he's used his credit card lately?" she asked.

He nodded and pulled out his phone. She watched him for a minute before she asked, "How are you able to check his credit card?"

Lincoln slanted her an almost sheepish look. "I know his password."

"How do you know his password?"

"He's used the same one on all his accounts since high school. The guy is as naive as it gets."

She chuckled and leaned over in an attempt to peer at his phone screen. "What's the password?"

He pulled the phone away. "I'm not going to tell you that. I might not be a good guy, but I'm not such a thoughtless bastard as to give out someone's password."

She huffed without any heat and waited as he pulled up Carter's credit card account.

"Okay," Lincoln said. "I don't know what's going on, but he booked a room at another hotel late last night. Hopefully he's still there. Let's go."

THE OTHER HOTEL WAS NEARBY, and it took very little time for Lincoln to charm an employee into giving him the room number and then talk his way into the room.

It was clear from the state of the room that Carter had spent the night in the room—evidently with a woman—but neither was there when they got in.

So they spent the next few hours searching the casinos and restaurants.

Summer was on the edge of crying as she wandered through room after room of crowds and noise and lights and chaos. She hated casinos now more than she ever had before.

She hated that Carter was here somewhere and they couldn't find him.

Finally, she talked to a nice middle-aged hostess who recognized the picture she showed her of Carter. The woman told her she thought he was in a small back room at an exclusive high-stakes poker game.

Naturally. Carter would be at the stupidest spot in the whole stupid place.

She texted Lincoln, who was searching another floor, saying she'd meet him there.

She got to the poker room easily, but it took a while for her to find the private back room. Lincoln had beaten her to it. He was talking to someone when she arrived, and then he came over to her with a frown.

"We can't get in unless we're playing. And we can't play without fronting the required money. So we'll probably just have to wait here until he comes out."

"But that might be hours. How much money?"

"Ten fucking thousand." Lincoln looked tired and bad-tempered, and his hair was a rumpled mess.

"Let's just pay it. I really don't want to wait for who knows how many more hours."

Lincoln's eyebrows shot up. "You know I'm a bartender, right? I don't have ten K just sitting in my bank account."

"I do. I'll pay it."

"But you'll have to go through a bunch of rigmarole to get that much from your trust fund, won't you?"

"Yeah, but I have a separate account where my salary goes in every month. I've never taken any out. I don't get paid much, but after six years it adds up. I have plenty there."

"You shouldn't have to use that much of your money just to—"

"Stop it, Lincoln. I'm tired of waiting. I want to find him now. I'll front the money if you'll play the game. I'm terrible at poker, as I'm sure won't surprise you. You can play, can't you?"

"Yeah. I can play." His eyes searched her face. "You sure? You might end up losing the money."

"Yes. I'm sure. We're doing this." She paused. "I will be allowed in with you, won't I?"

"Yeah. One observer is allowed." He put a hand on the middle of her back as they moved toward the entrance of the room.

"If he's not in this room, I'm seriously going to sit down on the floor and cry."

Lincoln's eyes were focused ahead of them as he murmured, "You and me both, baby. You and me both."

After she got the required money, they were let into the private room. It was a decent-sized room—much less crowded and overwhelming than the main rooms—and it featured four round tables. At present, three different games were going on. They were obviously not games open to the public. Lincoln had had to talk his way in.

She scanned the room until her eyes landed on Carter. He looked horrible in wrinkled clothes and a weekend's growth of beard and a debauched appearance that wasn't at all like him.

She gripped Lincoln's arm as he steered them toward that table.

Fortunately, there were two empty spots, so he'd be able to join Carter's game.

They'd almost reached the table when Carter's bleary eyes finally focused on them. His surprised and then aggrieved expression would have been amusing had they not gone through such an ordeal to find him.

"Go away," he told them.

"We're not going away. We've been looking for you for two days." Lincoln sounded cool. Slightly annoyed. He took the empty chair beside Carter. "Deal me in."

"Carter, please," Summer began, a note of obvious pleading in her tone.

Carter's eyes flashed to her and then back to Lincoln. "She can't be here."

She couldn't believe this was Carter. She'd never seen him like this before. "I'm standing right here. You can talk to me and not about me."

Carter ignored her and said to Lincoln, "She can't be here. If she stays, I'm gone. And you won't find me again."

The pain in her throat was so deep she raised a hand to span the base of her neck. "Wh-what?" She gave Lincoln an agonized look, instinctively seeking help from him.

Lincoln's features twisted briefly with something like sympathy as he stood back up and came toward her. "Why don't you wait outside?"

"What? No! I need to talk to him. Something's wrong. He needs—"

"I know he needs you." He was speaking low. Just to her. His hand was on her back again—comforting rather than guiding this time. "I know something's wrong. But if we push, we're going to lose him. He's going to let me stay, so let me try. You can go back to the hotel and rest."

"No! I'm not going to the room. If I have to, I'll wait outside. I'm not going to leave him. I'm not going to leave *you*."

"Okay. Then wait outside. Find somewhere comfortable to sit. Maybe get some food. It's going to be a while. I'll text and let you know how things are going."

She nodded, barely able to speak over the ache in her throat.

He cupped her face and met her eyes. "Trust me, Summer. I'll do everything I can to bring him back to you."

"Okay. I trust you." She sniffed and glanced over to Carter. He'd been watching them with a tense expression, but he looked quickly away when she met his eyes. "Is he mad at me? Have I done something wrong?"

"Shit, baby. Of course you haven't done anything wrong. I'll see if I can find out what's going on with him. Just give me some time."

"Okay." She wanted to hug Lincoln. She wanted him to hug her. But they didn't have that kind of relationship, so she squeezed his arm instead. "I'll leave and find somewhere to wait."

Walking out that room was one of the hardest things she could remember, but she did it.

She didn't have a choice.

6

SUMMER FOUND A PLACE TO SIT IN A LARGE OPEN HALLWAY THAT connected different rooms of the casino together. It wasn't exactly quiet, but it was as out of the way as she could find, and she'd have a view of Lincoln or Carter as they exited the main poker room.

She planted herself there with nothing but her phone to amuse herself. She sat. And she sat. And she sat.

For three hours she sat, until she was on the verge of either screaming or falling asleep. The only thing that kept her going was Lincoln's texts, which came in every fifteen or twenty minutes. They were never very informative, but he'd check in with her, make sure she was okay, and let her know he was still playing poker.

It was after one in the morning when she looked fuzzily in the direction of the poker room and saw Lincoln heading in her direction.

He looked just as tired and frustrated as she felt.

She jumped to her feet and hurried over, grabbing for his arm when she reached him. "Where's Carter?"

He shook his head. His jaw was clinched, and his forehead was damp.

"Lincoln, tell me what's going on."

"He's not coming," he gritted out. "We'll have to try again tomorrow."

She made a whimpering sound, but Lincoln looked so angsty—like he was holding so much emotion back—that she bit back her instinctive objection. She took his arm as he started walking, and they didn't talk as they rode in a cab back to their hotel and returned to their rooms.

She'd unlocked her door when she finally turned to Lincoln. "What happened? Please tell me."

"Nothing happened." His voice was low, hushed, angry. "I sat in that fucking chair for three hours and played round after round, and he wouldn't talk to me. Not a single, fucking word." The flat of his hand connected with the doorframe, and it looked like he'd been just planning to lean against it, but he hit the frame with such force it made a loud slapping sound. He removed his hand quickly and shook it like it hurt. "Damn it all."

Summer hated to see Lincoln like that. Not just angry but on the edge of defeat. She reached up to rub his shoulder. "It's not your fault. I don't know what's gotten into him, but we did the best we could today. We'll try again tomorrow. We'll get through to him eventually. I know we will."

He met her gaze with aching green eyes. "You think so?"

"Yes. I think so. Whatever's eating at Carter isn't going to be big enough to change who he is. He'll come around. I know he will. We'll try again tomorrow." She'd been just as upset as Lincoln was earlier, but she suddenly knew the words were true as she spoke them. She believed them, and they made her feel better.

Lincoln gave a long sigh, the tension releasing from his body with his breath. He looked down at where her hand was resting on his shirt, then lifted his eyes again as he reached up to brush a strand of hair behind her ear. "Okay. We'll try again tomorrow."

Her heart fluttered as she held his gaze. She was suddenly overwhelmed with the urge to kiss him, press herself against him, burrow into his heat, his strength, the deep feeling she could see on his face. She licked her lips and dropped her eyes.

Lincoln cleared his throat. "Okay. I'm sure you're exhausted. I'll let you get to bed. And I need about an hour-long shower."

She was turning toward the door when he added, "Oh wait. Here. This is yours." He handed her a wad of bills.

"What is this?"

"This is your money back. That you fronted for the game. Most of it anyway."

"You mean you didn't lose it all?"

He chuckled. "Why do you sound so surprised? I did okay. I almost broke even. You ended up losing about three hundred bucks."

"Just three hundred? That's nothing. Wow. You did great."

"Great would have been making you money."

"I didn't even consider that an option, so getting most of it back is amazing." She stared down at the stack of bills. "Thanks."

"You're welcome."

"Not just for the solid poker playing. For everything." She

reached up to touch his face before she realized it wasn't entirely appropriate for their relationship. "Thank you, Lincoln."

He nodded and dropped his eyes. "You're welcome."

She was about to stretch up and kiss him. She was seriously right on the edge. Everything inside her was screaming at her to do it, so much so that her hands were actually trembling with the effort it took to hold herself back. "Okay," she managed to rasp. "Good night. I think I might need an hour-long shower too."

He smiled and stepped back, making it easier for her to turn away from him, step into her hotel room, and close the door. She felt safer alone in her room, but she still wanted to kiss him just as much.

She did end up taking a long shower, cleaning herself up and then bringing herself to orgasm with her hand under the hot spray. The release helped to relax her, but it didn't make her want Lincoln any less. As she changed into her pajamas, she couldn't stop thinking about him.

She brushed her teeth. Brushed her hair. Applied moisturizer to her face and lotion to the rest of her body.

She was ready for bed. She was tired and needed sleep. But her mind was buzzing with a need that wouldn't be denied.

Seeing Lincoln would be enough. She didn't need to kiss him or have sex with him or anything like that. She just needed to see him once more before bed.

She knocked on the door that connected to his room.

"It's open, Summer," he called out. "What's the matter?"

She opened the door. As he'd said, the one on his side was hanging open so she could walk into his room.

She found him in front of the sink, his mouth full of toothpaste and wearing a pair of pajama pants.

He obviously had recently gotten out of the shower just like her.

Giving her a questioning look, he spit out his toothpaste and rinsed his mouth with water. "What's the matter?"

"Nothing. Just... checking on you. You were upset earlier." It was mostly true, and it sounded convincing.

He turned to face her, smelling clean and looking sexy as hell with his bare chest and low-riding pants. "I'm fine, Summer. Frustrated with my stubborn-ass brother, but that's not an unusual feeling. How are you?"

She came closer until she was standing only a few inches away. "I'm okay."

"Are you?"

"Frustrated just like you. Worried. But okay."

His eyes were searching her face almost urgently. "Did you really come in here just to check on me?"

She swallowed hard. "Uh, no. Not just for that."

"Then why?" His body was growing tenser. She could see it in the set of his shoulders and the clench of his jaw.

Suddenly nervous, she stared at the floor and tried to figure out what she should say.

He used one hand to tilt up her chin, so she couldn't hide her expression with her hair. "Summer?"

She tried to control her ragged breathing until she thought of something to say. "Your shower didn't last a whole hour. It's just been thirty minutes."

"I know that. Yours didn't last an hour either."

"I've never taken an hour-long shower in my life."

"Me either." He moved his hand slightly so he was

cupping her face. "Summer, tell me what you're doing here."

"I... I'm not sure I know. I just wanted to see you."

"Why?"

"Because... because I wanted to..."

There were no words. No words but the truth, and she couldn't get those out. But she couldn't fight the urge anymore. It was all consuming. Unstoppable.

She reached up to grab his face and pulled his head down into a kiss.

He stayed perfectly still for a few seconds, clearly taken by surprise. But then it was like a light switch had been flicked on inside him. He grabbed for her, tangling the fingers of one hand in her hair and wrapping the other arm around her waist. His mouth started to move urgently against hers, and it wasn't long until she felt his tongue.

It was so good—so exactly what she wanted—that she whimpered into the kiss and opened her mouth fully to his tongue. He stepped her backward until she connected with a wall, and the extra support was a relief because her knees were weak and Lincoln was all over her. His hands were moving greedily, touching her all over. He was making hungry sounds into the kiss, and they were really going to her head.

Her body throbbed with pleasure as her heart throbbed with something more, deeper.

She was dragging her fingernails down his bare back and trying to wrap one leg around him and sucking his tongue into her mouth again. She couldn't get enough, feel enough. She wanted so much more.

"Summer, baby," Lincoln murmured as he nibbled a line down her neck. "Tell me what you want."

"I want... this." She arched helplessly as her body pulsed with so much need and pleasure she could barely process it.

"But how much? How far?" He straightened up and met her gaze. His cheeks were flushed and his eyes almost wild. "I'll stop if you want me to—at any time you want me to—but I'm on the edge here, and it would help to know if I can really let myself go."

"You can," she whispered, taking his head in both hands. "You can let go. I want all of it."

He made a soft, rough groan and claimed her lips again. This time as he kissed, he gathered her up so she had to wrap her legs around his waist as he carried her to the bed. He leaned over to yank the coverlet off before he lowered her onto the sheet. Then he climbed on top of her and kissed her some more.

Despite his urgency, he didn't rush to the main event. He kissed her for a long time, and then his mouth moved farther down her body, kissing and caressing and pulling off her pajamas until she was naked and writhing beneath him.

She couldn't remember ever being so turned on before. The need was so strong it was almost aching. She tried to bite back the embarrassing sounds she was making, but she didn't have much success. She gasped and whimpered and made helpless mews as he teased her breasts with his lips and teeth and stroked her inner thighs.

Before she'd found any relief, he moved back up to her mouth and kissed her deeply again. She responded. She couldn't help but respond. But she was also rocking wantonly and trying to rub her aching arousal against one of his thighs.

"Lincoln," she gasped at last, tearing her mouth away from the kiss.

He raised himself up slightly so he could see her face. "What, baby?"

"I'm... I'm..."

"You're what?"

"I'm dying here! Are you torturing me on purpose?"

He choked on a laugh. "No. I'm just trying to control my impatience so I can make sure it's good for you."

"It's good for me. And I really need to come." She'd had good sex before, but she'd never been a particularly vocal person in the bedroom. She couldn't believe she'd actually said that out loud.

He chuckled as he pressed a brief, sweet kiss on her mouth. "Then why didn't you say so?"

She huffed and gave him an annoyed swat, but it did nothing to interfere with her arousal. She moaned long and low as he kissed his way down her body and then pulled her thighs apart to fit his head.

He held her open with his fingers and teased her clit, making her cry out at the sharp sensations. Then he sank two fingers inside her and pumped them as he continued to skillfully use his mouth.

She came in about ten seconds, arching up and clenching the sheet as the shudders ran through her. He didn't stop. He kept up his ministrations until she came again and then again. Her releases were loud and messy and completely uninhibited, and she was limp and breathless and ridiculously pleased with herself when he finally straightened up and slid his fingers—now soaking wet—from inside her.

He grinned down at her before he licked his fingers clean.

She frowned. "What are you smirking at?"

"It's not a smirk. It's a smile."

"It's a very smug smile, and I'm not sure I like it."

His eyes warmed even more as he lowered himself on top of her, his legs on either side of one of hers. "Yes, you do."

He was right. She did like it. She was having trouble holding back her own smile—not to mention a lot of giddy giggles. But she sniffed and said, "No, I don't. There's no call for you to look as smug as all that, just because you managed to get me off."

"I did more than get you off, and there's definitely cause for a little smugness." He kissed her almost gently, caressing her lips with his. "I didn't know you'd come so easily for me."

"Not that easy!" She didn't know why she was arguing. His teasing wasn't sharp or sarcastic. It was fond. Tender. It made her heart burst into flutters. "I don't come that easily!"

"You come very easy for me." He was still kissing her— light little brushes on her face and neck. "You were wet and ready for me after just a little bit of kissing. And your body responded to every way I touched you. You came three times for me just now, and we've barely gotten started." He moved his head lower and gave one of her nipples a big lick that made her cry out sharply. "Look at you. You're so responsive to me."

She was starting to shift restlessly beneath him again as a new coil of pleasure started to tighten between her legs. For some reason his husky voice was doing it for her as much as his touches. But there was a point to make here, and she wasn't going to give it up so easily. "Maybe I'm responsive to everyone."

"You don't think I'm going to believe that, do you? You're always so quiet and reserved. You're always completely in control of yourself. You're not like this with everyone. Something about me makes you let it go." He took her nipple between his teeth and gave it a little tug that made her arch her spine and give a little sob. "You're so good, baby. So beautiful. Look at how you let go for me. You're ready to come again, aren't you?"

She was. Despite her earlier release, her blood was coursing again. "Don't be cocky about it. I'm just really good at sex."

"I believe it. But I think you're particularly good with me." He tugged on her other nipple, causing her to make a loud sound and grab for the headboard to hold on. "Are you going to deny it?"

"Yes, I'm going to deny it." She was silly to be so stubborn. She knew it would be a challenge to him. But she couldn't help it. He might be smart and funny and sexy and softer than anyone she knew, but he was also unbelievably arrogant. And she didn't want him to have his way in this.

He was laughing as he kissed her lips. Then he mouthed his way down to her neck and sucked on the spot where her pulse was throbbing. He fit one hand between her legs until his thumb had found her clit. He rubbed it very lightly as he sucked.

She came again. Her body shook through it as she tried to muffle the sounds by biting her lower lip.

Thinking he'd proved his point, she let her body relax in the aftermath, but he kept rubbing and sucking until she came again, so hard she banged the headboard against the wall.

It was ridiculous.

Something was wrong with her. She'd always enjoyed sex, but she'd never come so easily or so much. She hadn't even known she could have so many orgasms in such a short space of time.

Maybe he was right. Her body was made just for him.

He was still shaking with soft amusement as he straightened up again. But his voice was almost awed as he said against her lips, "Oh baby, you're amazing. I've never known anyone like you."

She was trying to think of something to say in response when she felt him moving above her, and his erection brushed against her thigh through his thin pajama pants.

"You're kind of amazing yourself," she admitted, reaching for the waistband of his pants and starting to tug them down. "So maybe we can both be amazing together."

"I thought we just were amazing together."

"Well, yeah, but do you want to fuck me or not?"

"I definitely do." He got up and shucked his pants. Then walked to the sink and returned with a condom packet. He showed it to her. "Yes?"

"Yes," she said, relieved that he'd thought of it because she was so overwhelmed that she might not have.

He opened it quickly and rolled it on before he moved back onto the bed. He got on his knees between her legs and pulled her down toward him, raising her hips so she was aligned with him.

"What if I don't like this position?" she asked. She had no problems with the position even though it meant her less-than-perfect body was completely exposed to his view.

He quirked one corner of his mouth up, and his eyes raked up and down her body from her messy hair to her groin. "I think you will."

She tried to roll her eyes but got distracted when he

started to enter her. He didn't rush it. He sank into her with a series of slow thrusts and withdrawals, so the penetration was completely comfortable.

She squirmed when he was buried inside her completely. It was good. Tight. Incredibly hot. And she already needed more.

"How is it?" Lincoln asked breathlessly. He'd jerked his head to the side like he was trying to control himself.

"Good. Really good. I'm ready anytime you are."

He turned his head back, smiling as he looked her up and down again. "You're pink all the way to your stomach."

She managed to frown. "What's your point? My skin just does that."

"Yeah?"

"Yeah. It has nothing to do with any particular talent of yours."

"Okay." He was still smiling as he took his first thrust.

It felt so good she gasped and arched up, splaying her arms out to either side and fumbling for purchase on the bedding.

"No talent?" He was holding her ass in position, and it was a lot sexier than it should have been.

"No. You just moved your dick a little bit. That doesn't take talent."

He made several more thrusts in a row—harder and faster than before.

She sobbed in pleasure as her body shook and jiggled and tightened in growing pleasure.

Then he paused and met her eyes. "No talent?"

"No." She had to swallow over the word because she was desperate for more. "No... talent."

He started thrusting again, and this time he really went at it. He didn't stop, and he didn't slow. He took her exactly as she needed until she was tossing her head back and forth and babbling out pleas for him to make her come.

"You're gonna come," he muttered, thick and raspy. He was sweating and flushed just like she was, and his body was so tense it was almost shaking. But his motion never wavered, and his hands were strong and unrelenting as he held her in position. "You're gonna come so hard for me, baby. Don't hold back. Don't hold anything back from me. I want all of it."

She was choking on her sobs now, clutching at anything she could grab as her body was wracked by growing pleasure.

"You're so hot, baby. So beautiful. Look at you letting go for me. Don't fight it. Just let it come. You're going to feel so good."

She was feeling good. And agonized at the same time. She was way too loud for a hotel as the sensations finally peaked. Then she was coming hard.

He was still talking her through it. "There you go. So good. Don't hold anything back."

The pleasure lasted a long time, and she was limp at the end of it. Lincoln gently lowered her bottom back onto the bed, letting himself slip out from her as he repositioned them.

She was still trying to catch her breath as he checked the condom and then settled between her legs again, sinking inside her in a different position. She was really tight. Sensitized. But she loved how he felt inside her, and her body easily adjusted again.

He kissed her softly and then nuzzled her neck. "You okay?"

"I'm better than okay. I was lying before. You're definitely uniquely talented."

He laughed and kissed her again. "I do okay, but it's not really me. It's just us. We're in sync somehow."

"Yeah." She smiled up at him. "I think we are. Aren't you ready to come yourself?"

"Honestly, I'm about to lose it at any moment."

"Then come. Come now." She wrapped her arms around his neck, enjoying the weight of his body in this position. "I want you to."

"Okay."

He started to rock over her, and she bent her legs up so she'd have some leverage to meet his thrusts with her hips. They moved together rhythmically for a while until she could see him start to lose control.

She squeezed her inner muscles around him and intensified her motion.

He groaned and closed his eyes as his tempo accelerated.

Soon they were moving fast and hard and urgent, and she could feel the tension building in his body until it finally broke.

He'd been making soft grunts as he thrust, but now he made a choking sound and froze for a few seconds before he rode out his climax with a long, soft groan.

She could see the release washing over his face. She could feel his body softening afterward.

And she loved it.

She loved all of it.

It was the best sex she'd ever had.

After a minute of recovering himself, Lincoln went to throw the condom away, wash up, and go to the bathroom.

When he returned, she only had a few seconds to leer at his naked body—long limbs, broad shoulders, attractive muscle development in his arms, abs, and thighs—before he pulled back on his pajama pants.

He lay down next to her, his eyes running up and down her body and a little smile on his lips.

Suddenly self-conscious, she pulled the top sheet over herself.

"Why did you do that?" he asked, sounding faintly disapproving.

"Because I don't like to lie around naked when I'm not actively having sex. Especially with you peering at me that way."

"I wouldn't peer at you if I didn't love how you look." He reached over to stroke her still warm cheek. "Naked or not."

That was kind of sweet. She felt a little melty but tried to fight it. Melty feelings toward Lincoln Wilson couldn't be wise.

"You can sleep in here tonight if you want," he added. "Or go back to your own room if you'd rather. Whatever you'd prefer."

"At the moment, I can't even move, much less make those kinds of decisions."

He chuckled. "You want me to turn out the lights?"

"Might as well."

He turned off the bedside lamp and then the lights over the bathroom vanity. It was dark in the room as he returned, settling beside her and pulling the covers halfway up his chest. He rolled onto his side to face her. "You feel okay about everything?"

She glanced at him in surprise. "Yeah. I feel fine. I mean,

pretty good after all that great sex. And kind of tired. And a little guilty that I forgot about Carter for a while. Still worried about him. But fine."

He touched her hand under the sheet. "You don't have to feel guilty about Carter."

"Don't you?"

"Yeah. I do. But that doesn't mean you should. You didn't do anything wrong. He's made his own choices. We can make our own choices too."

"I know that's true. But I still feel... I don't want him to find out about this."

Lincoln was quiet for a little longer than normal conversation called for. Then he said, "Yeah. If this was just a onetime thing, no reason why he needs to know."

She didn't like the sound of that.

She didn't want this to be a onetime thing.

But the idea of Carter finding out that she'd fucked his older brother was enough to make her stomach churn, so surely it made more sense for this to be a random one-night stand.

It had been good. Incredible, really. But that didn't mean it was intended to last.

That conclusion gave her enough energy to get up, grab her pajama set from the floor, and carry it with her to the bathroom. There, she peed and cleaned up and got dressed. When she was done, she meant to head back to her own room and her own bed.

But it felt like Lincoln was watching her in the dark as she emerged from the bathroom, and something unspoken in his mood led her back to his bed instead.

"Too exhausted to make it back to my bed," she said lightly, trying to dispel any significance from her decision.

"Well, we had a long day and quite a workout. No one can blame you for that." It sounded like he was smiling beside her.

Then he reached over and pulled her against his side. She snuggled up, really liking how it felt there with his arm wrapped around her.

She fell asleep in just a couple of minutes.

She woke up the next morning, knowing she'd slept too late even before her eyes landed on the bedside clock that read 10:25.

She sat up and blinked around. She was still in Lincoln's room. It looked the same as it had the night before. But Lincoln wasn't there.

"Lincoln?" she called out, in case he was in the bathroom or in her room that was connected by an open doorway.

He didn't answer. He wasn't there.

He'd gone somewhere. For some reason the idea made her stomach sink. She tried to talk herself out of it. She'd slept really late. He'd probably just run downstairs for breakfast or to work out. Yes, they'd had sex last night, but a one-night stand certainly didn't require him to hang around bored until she managed to wake up.

There was no reason to feel lonely and disappointed.

She shifted on the bed, recognizing how sore she was after the sex they'd had last night. Then she flopped back down onto the pillow and stared at the ceiling, trying to figure out how she felt and what it all meant.

She'd come to no answers when the door opened and Lincoln came into the room, dressed in jeans and a gray T-shirt and carrying a paper bag and two cups of coffee.

She sat back up, pulling up on the straps of her tank top that had flopped down past her shoulder.

"Hey," Lincoln said. "You're awake."

"I'm awake. I didn't mean to sleep so long."

"I just woke up an hour ago. Got some coffee and a breakfast sandwich if you want it."

"Thank you!" She reached for the coffee and tasted it, pleased to discover it already had the right amount of cream in it.

Lincoln came over and sat on the edge of the bed near where she was sitting. He scanned her face as he sipped his own coffee, and something about the look felt significant.

"What is it?" she asked.

"I talked to Carter."

"You did? When?"

"Just now. I took a chance and pounded on his door, and he was there."

"How is he?"

"He's a wreck, as you'd expect. But he's sober now, and at least he's willing to talk."

"What did he say?"

"Not much. He's mad that I brought you here."

"I brought *you* here."

"Yeah, I didn't try to explain that to him. I'd rather him be angry with me than angry with you. He's used to that. But I think he'll be open to talking to you if you want to do that."

She jumped out of bed, wincing just slightly at the way the muscles in her stomach stretched. "Yes. Definitely. I'll run and get dressed and go see him right away before he changes his mind and leaves the room."

"I don't think he'll be leaving anytime soon. He's seriously a wreck. You can probably take your time."

She was already hurrying to her room with her coffee. "I don't want to take my time. I want to go now. I'm just going to throw my clothes on."

She had second thoughts after she'd closed the connecting door, so she pushed it back open, ran back to where Lincoln still sat on the bed, and reached into the bag for one of the wrapped sandwiches, taking it with her as she returned to her room.

Ten minutes later, she and Lincoln were riding the elevator up a couple of floors to Carter's room.

She was anxious. Jittery. When the doors opened, she reached out to take Lincoln's hand as they walked down the hall. She didn't even think about it. She just needed reassurance, and she knew she could get it from him.

He didn't act like the gesture was strange. He held her hand until they reached Carter's room. Then she let his slip from her grip as she knocked on the door.

"Go away, Lincoln," Carter's muffled voice called out. "I don't need a babysitter."

"It's not Lincoln."

There was silence from the room. But after a minute the door swung open.

Lincoln had been right. Carter was wrecked. He wore a pair of old sweats and nothing else. He still hadn't shaved, so he had at least four days' worth of beard. His eyes were bleary, and his skin was too pale.

The only time she'd ever seen him looking so bad before was when he'd had a killer case of the flu.

He stared at her with reddened brown eyes.

"Can I come in and talk?" she asked at last.

She wasn't sure how he was going to answer for a few seconds, but then he finally nodded. He stepped out of the doorway to let her in.

She glanced back at Lincoln. "I'm going to talk to him for a few minutes."

"Okay." Lincoln's expression was uncharacteristically quiet, like he'd somehow sucked all of his vibrant personality deep inside. His eyes moved between her face and Carter's. "I'll wait out here. Let me know if you need anything."

She was about to tell him that he didn't need to wait for her, but she changed her mind. They didn't need any distractions from Carter right now. Besides, the knowledge of Lincoln outside the room if she needed him made her feel better.

She walked in. Carter closed the door behind them. She turned to face him and had no idea what to say. To give herself something to do, she went and sat on the foot of the bed. The room smelled like sweat and liquor. It wasn't really what she wanted to smell after the long night she'd had, but it was the least of her worries at the moment.

Carter came over and sat beside her. "Sorry about last night. About how I acted."

She nodded, a tension relaxing in her chest at the words

and at the sound of his voice. He sounded like the Carter she'd known and loved all her life. "It's okay."

"It's not okay." He was staring down at the floor. "I'm a mess. I screwed up. I really screwed up."

"It doesn't matter. Everyone screws up sometimes. It doesn't change who you are or how we feel about you."

He shot her a quick look. "I lost a shitload of money this weekend. Way more than we can afford."

"That doesn't matter either. When the acquisition goes through, Wilson Hotels will be making a profit again, and your finances will turn around."

"I dropped the ball on work too."

"Then you can pick it up again. You didn't do anything that can't be fixed, Carter."

He was still staring at the floor, chewing on his lower lip.

"Carter, what's the matter? Why can't we just shrug this off and move on?"

He shook his head and muttered, "I've been so stupid. I should have... I didn't realize... And now it's too late."

She had no idea what he was talking about, but she didn't like the desperation in his tone. She wrapped one arm around his shoulders. "It's not too late, Carter. So you went on a major binge this weekend and you wasted some money. It happens. People do it all the time. And anyone who would judge you harshly for it needs to do some self-reflection and ask themselves if they have any cause to be so self-righteous. People mess up. Even good people. It doesn't change who you are, and it's not going to stop you from getting what you want out of life."

He turned his head and gazed at her with a look that was too poignant, too aching.

She gulped. "Carter, please tell me. What's the matter? What's hurt you so much?"

He opened his mouth like he would say something but then gave his head a firm shake.

Her shoulders drooped a little, but she didn't want to risk pushing right now. "Okay. You don't have to tell me right now. I hope you'll tell me eventually, but that's up to you. I'm really sorry, Carter."

"What are you sorry for?"

"For always acting like you're supposed to be perfect. Just because you're always so good and strong and I've always been able to depend on you, I sometimes forget that you're not... not a saint. I hope I didn't make things harder for you."

He reached up and touched her cheek very lightly before dropping his hand. "You don't make anything worse, Summer. I'm the one who screwed up. And the truth is I like for you to think of me that way. I want to be that man for you."

"But you're a human being like everyone else, and it's wrong for me to not let you be. I'll be a better friend to you, Carter. I promise I will." She leaned her head against his shoulder in a companionable gesture and was relieved when he wrapped an arm around her. He didn't smell very good, but it was comforting anyway.

"Shit," he muttered, not pulling away from her. "I hate this crash back to the real world. I hate feeling like such a failure."

"Everyone hates feeling that way, but it's not that big a deal. We're the only ones who know what happened this weekend. No one else does. Not even your mom. And we love you, Carter. We're not going to change how we feel about you."

"We?"

"Me and Lincoln." She raised her eyes to his face and saw a strange expression there. "He does love you, Carter. He really does. And he's been great for the past few days, helping me find you. I couldn't have done it without him."

"Yeah." The one word sounded faint, utterly exhausted.

"So will you come home now? Will you come home with us?"

He hesitated just a minute. Then, "Yeah. Yeah, I will."

THEY GOT BACK to Green Valley after dinner that evening. The three of them. They had a quick bite to eat when they got home, and then they went their separate ways to their rooms. Mrs. Wilson was still on her trip to the south of France, so she wasn't around.

All of them were tired, and none of them really knew what to say.

It was enough that Carter was home now. They could fix everything else after a good night's sleep.

Summer was sore and felt kind of gross from the flight, so she took a long bubble bath in the big tub in her bathroom. Then she put on a little knit gown and rubbed on vanilla-scented lotion.

She was exhausted and restless at the same time.

She knew what she wanted.

She wanted Lincoln.

It felt like she needed him.

But they'd agreed it was just a one-night stand, and she could hardly go pounding on his door and begging him to fuck her again.

Or what was worse, begging him to cuddle her. She wanted that just as much as sex.

She rubbed lotion into her legs for longer than normal, trying to work through her feelings so she could go to sleep like the good, reasonable person she'd always been.

When there was a knock on the door, she jumped.

The knock had come from the connecting door. Flutters broke out in her chest.

"It's open," she called.

The doorknob jiggled. "No, it's not."

She jumped up and hurried to unlock the door. "Sorry," she said, swinging it open. "They must have locked it when they cleaned in here."

"Yeah. My side was locked too." He'd obviously just gotten out of the shower. He smelled like soap, and he wore nothing but his pajama pants.

They stared at each other over the threshold. Summer had no idea what to say, but her blood was starting to throb in her veins.

"I was just checking on you," he said at last.

"Oh. I'm okay."

"Are you?"

"Yeah. Are you?"

"I guess."

They stared at each other again.

Eventually the compulsion was simply too strong. There was no way to stop the words from her throat. "Did you... did you want to come in?"

Something broke on Lincoln's face. "Is that what you want?"

"Yeah. Yeah. I do. I really want that." She stepped out of the doorway. "So... please."

He made a rough sound in his throat as he stepped into her room. Then he grabbed her urgently, pulling her into a hungry kiss that ended with him picking her up and carrying her to her bed.

He didn't leave her room for the rest of the night.

7

―――――

Later that week, on Saturday evening, Summer walked into Lincoln's bar, feeling self-conscious and just a little excited.

Lincoln's week off had ended yesterday, so he was back at work this evening. He'd suggested that she should stop by the bar tonight to see him. When she'd assumed he was teasing and responded accordingly, he'd made it clear he was serious.

He really wanted her to stop by.

And the truth was she wanted to see him too. She'd gotten used to spending her evenings with him for the past week, and she didn't like that he was suddenly gone for so many hours at night.

In order to preserve her sense of self-sufficiency, she'd come up with a good excuse. Mrs. Wilson had returned from France today, tanned and relaxed and overflowing with herb and lavender concoctions to gift her family and friends with. She'd blithely given Summer and Lincoln a quaint newlywed basket filled with herbal sachets, lavender spray for the bridal bed, and scented oil intended for *sensual pleasure*.

Summer had thanked Mrs. Wilson profusely when she'd received the basket since it was fresh and pretty. But when she'd started to dig into the contents of the basket, her eyes had bugged out of her head.

Surely Mrs. Wilson hadn't actually paid attention to the specific items included. A mother wasn't likely to give sensual massage oil to her son and daughter-in-law. She'd probably just seen the word "newlywed" and thought it was pretty and so had gotten it for them.

After her initial shock, Summer had started to giggle, and she hadn't been able to stop.

So she returned the items to the little basket and put the basket back into the gift bag and then carried it with her to the bar so she could see Lincoln's face as he opened it.

Because she'd grown up in Green Valley and the town was a particularly insular community, Summer saw people she knew whenever she went out. Tonight was no exception. She saw a few of her former classmates as soon as she entered the bar, so she stopped to chat with them for a minute.

She glanced over a couple of times toward Lincoln, who was pouring out beers for a large group of young guys who must have just arrived. He'd obviously spotted Summer. He wasn't looking at her, but his mouth had turned up in a familiar little smirk.

Like he was pleased with himself for getting her to come visit him.

Summer wasn't as annoyed by the smirk as she should have been. In fact, it filled her with a possessive kind of excitement. Like that smug, handsome man behind the bar was hers.

He *was* her husband. Legally, officially, her husband. They were both wearing rings to prove it.

When she finished talking, she went over to the bar and took an empty stool, putting the gift bag on the counter and waiting until Lincoln was done with the guys.

It only took a minute for him to saunter over to her. He leaned over the bar to kiss her. It was probably just to confirm their role as a newly married couple, but it made her blush anyway.

"You want something different to drink this evening?" he asked her. "What about an amaretto sour?"

"Yeah, that would be good. I haven't had one of those for a while."

"What's in the bag?"

"That's for us from your mom. Wait until you see it."

His eyes narrowed on her mischievous expression. "I guess this is going to be good. Give me just a minute."

He made her drink and then a couple of cosmos for two women who'd just come in. Then there was a lull, so he came back over and opened the bag.

He pulled out the basket, his eyes laughing and curious. Summer waited with held breath as he pulled one item after another out of the carefully displayed arrangement. "Oh perfect. This is just like her." He held a sachet up to his nose and reared back quickly at the scent. "What are we supposed to do with these things?"

"Put them in our drawers to make our underwear smell nice."

"I don't want my underwear to smell like a spice rack. She's out of her mind. What is this?" He pulled out the oil.

Summer waited, her mouth twitching just slightly.

"Oh my fucking God," he breathed, his eyes widening as he read the label of the bottle.

"Very thoughtful of her, wasn't it? She must want to spice up our sex life with lavender and cinnamon-scented sensual massages."

Lincoln made a choking sound. Then he put down the bottle and burst into laughter. People around them turned to look, but no one appeared surprised. They were married, after all. It must seem natural that they'd be laughing together.

"She couldn't possibly have known that was in here," he said.

"I hope not. I know she's not any sort of prude, but I can't imagine her giving that oil to her son."

"I don't think I'll mention it to her."

"Definitely not. No need to embarrass her. It was a nice thought, I suppose, especially since she definitely must suspect that our marriage isn't exactly..."

"Yeah. She knows." Lincoln's expression quieted a bit as he continued, "But she's seen people get married for much worse reasons. Green Valley folks marry for money and business connections and to get around inheritance prohibitions all the time."

"I know." Summer did know. She'd always suspected that their friends Lance and Savannah had gotten married because of a provision in Lance's grandmother's will. She didn't know specifics, but she'd heard plenty of rumors. It was their business, and it had clearly worked out well for them. The two were obviously completely in love now.

People in Green Valley did things that would have seemed

crazy in a different place. Money always changed the way people made life decisions.

"I've got to get back to work," Lincoln said in a different tone, turning to look at a group who was entering the bar. "Hang out for a while."

"Why?"

"Because I like having you here." He slanted her a flirtatious look. "And it gives me something good to look at."

She rolled her eyes at him.

He leaned over and murmured in her ear, "And if you stay up late enough, we can try out that massage oil after I get off."

She went home after a couple of hours and hung out with Carter and Mrs. Wilson, who were watching TV in the media room. She didn't go up to her room until almost midnight, and when she got there, she decided to take a bath.

So she had a long, relaxing soak in the tub with a candle and a glass of wine. Then she changed into a little nightgown and climbed into Lincoln's bed.

No reason not to wait for him there.

She fell asleep but woke up again when she felt him climb into bed beside her.

Smiling, she scooted over toward him, pressing herself against his warm body. It didn't take long for her to realize he was naked. "What?" She blinked and pulled the covers down to verify what she'd felt. She hadn't been very deeply asleep, and Lincoln's familiar, sexy presence in bed had woken her all the way up.

He chuckled and pulled her into a loose hug. "What, what?"

"Why aren't you wearing any clothes?"

"Figured it would save us time later. You were planning to take my clothes off eventually, weren't you?"

She kissed his chest. Then his neck. Then his mouth. "Probably. But no reason for you to be presumptuous about it."

"But presumptuousness is one of my strongest qualities." He smelled clean. He'd obviously taken a quick shower after work.

"Hmm. That's true. You really shouldn't be rewarded for that particular quality." She ran her hands up and down his body, delighting in the firm, rippling contours and flat planes of his form and finally ending on his erection, which was already mostly hard.

He sucked in a sharp breath and shifted his hips slightly as she stroked him. "That feels kind of like reward to me."

"Does it?" She moved one of her hands down so she could massage his balls, delighted when he moaned in naked pleasure.

"Fuck, yeah. If you're trying to punish me for my presumptuousness, I might suggest a different strategy."

"I'm not really into punishment, if you want to know the truth."

"I know you're not," he murmured thickly, gently brushing her hair back behind her shoulder so it wasn't blocking her face. "You're the sweetest thing I've ever known." His face twisted as she intensified her intimate massage.

She was getting really turned on by his responsiveness to her, how easily she was turning him on. And her heart was doing something else from his words. Something just as strong.

She moved one hand to caress his belly as she lightened her touch to a brush of her fingers up and down his shaft. She leaned down to kiss his neck, trailing her mouth down to one of his nipples.

"Fuck, baby, I love how you touch me. I love—" He broke off with a gasp when she lowered her head even farther to lick a line up the underside of his erection. His hips bucked off the bed as she sucked hard on the tip.

She was grinning when she let him slip from her mouth, but she didn't have a chance to gloat about her victory for long. His expression shifted to something hot and feral as he grabbed her and flipped them both over.

He started on her body, tugging off her nightgown and then kissing and caressing her the way she had him. Soon she was just as shamelessly turned on as he was, writhing beneath him and begging for him to make her come.

Once he'd gotten her into the state he wanted her, he turned her over onto her hands and knees and fucked her vigorously from behind. He made her come repeatedly, and it was so intense that she had to hide her face in a pillow so she wouldn't be heard outside the room.

She'd never been loud in bed. Not until she'd had sex with Lincoln. It was almost embarrassing how completely he could make her let go.

When they'd both had enough, he'd turned her over onto her back and positioned them so her legs were wrapped high around his back. They rocked together slowly, kissing a lot, completely wrapped up in each other. Lincoln was beyond words now, but his eyes were speaking. He was with her. All the way.

Summer had never felt so close to another person.

Not once in her life.

Lincoln took his time, but he finally came—hard and almost desperate as the spasms of release shuddered through him. It took him a while to recover afterward, so Summer found the energy to take care of the condom and go to the bathroom to pee and clean up.

She returned to bed, pleased when Lincoln pulled her over to snuggle beside him.

"We forgot to use the sensual massage oil," she said after a few minutes.

He gave a huff of what sounded like exhausted amusement. "We sure did. Just as well. Not sure I want my bed smelling like all that stuff."

"If you check out your underwear drawer, you'll find I put all the sachets in there, so your underwear should smell particularly good tomorrow."

"You did not," he said slowly.

Summer giggled.

He stroked her hair with a chuckle. "You shouldn't tease your husband like that."

"What? You tease me all the time!"

"That's a husband's prerogative."

"That doesn't make any sense. If you have a husband's prerogative to tease me, then I have a wife's prerogative to tease you." Something about the words sounded significant. Like she was staking a claim on him. And she wasn't sure she was in the position to do that even though she wanted to. So she added in a different tone, "Anyway, you were teasing me long before we were married."

"That's true." His hand was still lightly running down the length of her loose hair. "Maybe I thought you needed it."

"Why would I need it?"

"Because you never really had a family to tease you. And for a while Carter was your only real friend. He always treated you like you were delicate. Like you were made of glass. I knew you were stronger than that. So maybe I wanted to do something to provoke you."

She lifted her head since she was genuinely interested in what he was saying—and also very touched. "Really? What did you want to provoke me to do?"

"Show me who you really are. How strong you really are. You've always hid it from the world. And I wanted to see it."

She checked his face in the mostly dim light of the room, and she could see that he was serious. He was telling her the truth. Her cheeks burned because it felt like he was seeing deep inside her, all the way to her soul. She nuzzled his neck, partly to hide her face from him. "And what do you think now that you see it?"

Her hair had moved with her new position, so now he was rubbing her bare back. "I think it's the biggest victory of my life."

She had to check his expression again to make sure he wasn't teasing. He smiled at her but not with irony. She hid her face again.

He laughed softly as he kept rubbing her back.

It felt like he might say something else. Something that would change things. Something that might terrify her.

But when he spoke again, it was casually. "So what did you do with the rest of the evening?"

Summer was both relieved and disappointed by the loss of the moment before. She managed to answer naturally enough. "I hung out with Carter and your mom. Just watching TV."

"How did Carter seem?"

"Better. More like himself. It still feels like there's some distance between us that wasn't there before, but he's definitely better than he was. Have you talked to him?"

"Just about business stuff and everyday stuff. Nothing deep."

"So you still don't know what happened to make him lose it last weekend?"

"No. And I guess you don't either."

"No, I don't. I wish I did. It's got to be big to push Carter into something like that. I really feel like we need to know what it is so we can help him if he has to deal with it again."

"He'll tell us eventually."

"Will he? He's not really much of a sharer. At least he never shared stuff easily with me. Deep, personal stuff, I mean."

"He never shared much with me either. He's pretty reserved. But I think he'll tell us when he's ready. Even things he tries to hold back will come out eventually." He sighed and shifted slightly, like he'd remembered something he didn't want to.

"What are you thinking of?" she asked, idly fondling one of his biceps.

"A big fight we had several years ago. He was trying to

hide from himself how mad he was at me, but it came out eventually."

"What did you do?"

Lincoln grew still. Didn't answer.

"Is it the thing that he owes you for?"

"Yes."

"What is it? What did you do?" She felt urgent—like she really wanted to know whatever bad thing Lincoln had done to Carter that made him owe him so much—but she kept her voice casual because it felt like Lincoln would clam up if she pushed too hard.

"It's a long, ugly story. You don't really need to know it."

"But I want to know it. I can't believe something so big happened to Carter and he never told me about it."

"I asked him not to."

"Why did you do that?" She lifted her head to frown down at Lincoln in confusion.

He licked his lips. Glanced away. "Because I didn't want you to know. I'm not proud of it. And I don't want you to know."

"So you're not going to tell me even now?"

He met her eyes again, and for a moment she thought he would relent. But then he shook his head. "No. I know how much you love Carter, and I don't want you to hate me for hurting him." When she started to object, he added quickly, "I didn't mean to hurt him. I never meant to hurt Carter. But I did just the same. And I really don't want you to start hating me again."

"I don't think I would hate you. That was in the past. You've changed. And I don't think I would hate you now."

He kissed her cheek. Then her mouth. Then the curve of her neck. "I'm not going to risk it."

She gave up arguing. Carter had refused to tell her, and now Lincoln was too. Maybe she'd find out eventually, but it was obviously a secret between the two of them, and it didn't seem respectful to pry.

Things were good right now. She could enjoy being with Lincoln. Things were improving with Carter. And maybe things could get even better later on.

She'd had incredible sex tonight—better than she'd known she was capable of having—and her body was still deliciously sated from all the orgasms Lincoln had given her. She felt close to him emotionally too. He was still holding her against him even as his eyes closed and his body relaxed.

She was ready to sleep. And for right now she was allowed to sleep with her husband.

And something about what he'd said to her earlier rang true. She felt stronger—more herself—now than she'd been before she'd married him.

She wasn't going to get uptight about the things she didn't know.

A WEEK AFTER THAT, Summer woke up and didn't know if she was in her bed or Lincoln's. Since they'd been spending every night together now, she was getting used to waking up with him, but sometimes they spent the night in her room and sometimes in his.

She raised her head and blinked around, realizing that they were in her room. He'd worked a late shift at the bar last night, and so she'd been asleep when he'd gotten in. She'd woken up when he climbed into her bed.

She'd thought he'd wanted sex, so she'd tried some sleepy kissing. On other nights after his shift, it hadn't taken her long to wake up. He'd kissed her back but then had settled her at his side and told her to go back to sleep. She had. So they hadn't had sex at all last night.

There were certain challenges in being in a sexual relationship with a man who worked entirely different hours than her.

Today was Saturday morning, which was why her alarm hadn't gone off. Pleased with that realization, she relaxed back into the bed, turning her head to see Lincoln sprawled out beside her.

He always got hot at night. She considered that a good thing since she could snuggle up against him at any hour of the night and instantly get warm. But if he got too hot, he would push her away from him in his sleep and then push down the covers.

He must have gotten hot sometime during the night. The covers were down at his thighs, and he'd rolled all the way to the edge of the bed. Basically as far from her as he could get.

She giggled stupidly at the way he was practically clinging to the side of the bed.

She'd had a really good two weeks since they'd returned from Atlantic City. Far better than she would have expected when she'd first realized she was going to marry Lincoln Wilson.

The sex was good. Really good. Lincoln was attentive and creative and evidently an overachiever when it came to the bedroom. One silly part of her wanted to brag to the rest of the world about the fantastic sex she was having with him, but they'd been keeping it a secret.

Carter had mostly gone back to his regular self. He went into the office and didn't get drunk and hung out with his friends and went out on the occasional date. But it still felt like he was holding something back from her, and that was the only real worry that diminished her enjoyment of the past twelve days.

She settled back under the covers and managed to doze off lightly, but she wasn't sound asleep enough to not feel when Lincoln's body shifted the mattress. Peering out of squinted eyelids, she tried to discreetly observe him. He was lying on his back, idly scratching his chest.

Without warning, he turned his head toward her and said, "Hoping to catch me doing something embarrassing?"

She huffed. "How did you know I was awake?"

"I have a sixth sense."

"Well, it's a pretty creepy sixth sense. You always know when I'm in the room too—even if your back is to me. Like when I found you in the library. That day. You know."

"Of course I know that day." He reached out and rubbed her cheek with his knuckles. "I made you so mad you slapped me and then threw up."

"I didn't just throw up because I was mad at you. I'd also had a really bad headache all day."

His expression was soft. Slightly thoughtful. Definitely fond. She'd never dreamed Lincoln would look at her in that particular way. "Did you?"

"Yes, I did. No matter what your ego dictates, you aren't so important that you can make me sick with just a few mean words."

"It was more than a few mean words. I was terrible to you."

"You were also telling me the truth. I think... It doesn't make it right. I mean, you were a huge dick and you should definitely feel bad about it. But I think I needed to hear what you said to me that day. I think it helped me."

"Really?" His eyes were way too green—too vivid to be real—in the morning light.

"Yes, really. I'd been holding on to a lot of silly daydreams. I outgrew them long ago, but I was still holding on for some reason. I needed to let them go." She cleared her throat as she realized how vulnerable she was making herself. "They weren't... they weren't me anymore."

"No," he murmured, his fingers still playing gently with the hair falling over her cheek. "They weren't. You're way too good—too beautiful and strong and smart and sexy and incredible—to spend your life waiting for a certain man to notice you, especially when that man is as blind as my brother."

"I don't think I was throwing my life away though. I've done a lot. I've had a good life. I didn't let any lingering daydreams hold me back. I don't think I was that stupid."

"You weren't stupid at all." His voice was as hushed as hers was, as if someone might be able to overhear them. "But you couldn't see anyone but him. For a long time you couldn't see anyone but him."

The conversation was getting too intimate, too intense. It was making her head buzz and her breath quicken. With a vague hope of breaking the tension, she teased him. "Is that your way of indicating that you wanted to have sex with me before now and I was never interested?"

He laughed, but his expression didn't falter. He was cupping her cheek now. Like it was precious. "I've wanted to have sex with you for a very long time, but that wasn't what I meant. I meant you had your heart on reserve. For him. And you deserve better than that."

She nodded, acknowledging the truth to his words and also the sincerity with which he spoke them. "Thank you." Then, because nerves were quickly swallowing up her excitement, she added in a different tone, "So how long have you wanted to have sex with me?"

His tone and expression changed too, transforming back into his typical teasing irony. "You don't want to know the answer to that question."

"Why not? Would it creep me out? You weren't lusting for me back in high school, were you?"

"Give me a little credit. I might have noticed your body a few times, but that was pure natural instinct I wasn't in control of. I wasn't creeping on you."

"What did you notice about my body?" She was feeling better now. This kind of interaction was familiar. Fun. Safe. It didn't threaten to swallow her whole.

"Well." He rolled over so he was propped above her. He carefully pulled down the covers to expose her wrinkled gown. "I noticed your legs when you wore those shorts."

"What shorts?"

"You know what shorts."

She did know, and she couldn't help but giggle with pleasure.

"And you had a bad habit of wearing tops that showed off these." He brushed his fingertips over her breasts through the cotton of her gown. "It was highly disturbing to my equilibrium since you were supposed to be just my brother's pesky little friend."

"Oh. I didn't think you noticed me at all, except to make fun of me."

"I did notice. The truth is I'd always liked you and thought you deserved a lot more attention than you got. You were always hiding in corners. It bothered me."

"I was not hiding in corners!"

"Yes, you were. In fact, I'm pretty sure I found you in a few corners over the years."

He was right. Both about her staying away from the center of attention and about his happening upon her when she was lurking on the outskirts. Every time he had, he'd said something to annoy her, and she'd returned to hang out with her friends to get away from him.

"But I never wanted more than that from you. Not until you were back from college. Because then you were suddenly all grown up and even more gorgeous than ever. And still hiding in corners."

"I was not!" She glared but without much heat. "If you really wanted to have sex with me, then you went about it with entirely the wrong strategy. You could have been nice to me, you know."

He snorted. "Right. Because you'd be likely to jump into bed with Carter's brother, just because he was nice to you."

She thought about that and concluded he was right. "No. I wouldn't have. I never would have had sex with you if we hadn't been stuck in this weird situation."

"That's what I thought." He didn't look surprised or upset or disturbed by her comment. He looked slightly amused and slightly resigned.

"But if I hadn't been stuck in this weird situation, I would have missed out on something incredibly good. So things worked out pretty damn good as far as I'm concerned."

He smiled and moved farther over her so he could lean down and kiss her. "I think so too."

They kissed for a while until she became aware of a pressing issue that needed to be dealt with before they went any further. She pushed him away gently and, at his frown, explained, "I've got to run to the bathroom before we do anything. I'm not a fan of sex while needing to pee."

He laughed and rolled off her. She could feel him watching her as she got off the bed and walked to the bathroom. When she returned, he was still smiling, his eyes soft and fond as they rested on her face.

"What?" she demanded, torn between fluttery sentiment and self-consciousness.

"I don't know what that question is in reference to." Despite his dry tone, his expression was still that heart-stopping tender one as he rolled over her again.

"That question is in reference to your staring at me that way."

"What way?" He brushed little kisses all over her face and down to her neck.

She giggled because it felt so good—inside and out. "You know what way. You're supposed to be all cool and sarcastic. You're not supposed to look like that."

He was looking more like that than ever as he lifted his head to gaze down at her. "You still haven't explained the nature of the look you're taking issue with," he murmured before kissing her again.

She returned the kiss with enthusiasm, but then he broke

it with an expression that made it clear he was waiting for an answer. "I don't want to explain," she admitted, tucking her head after feeling her cheeks warm.

He turned her head so she was meeting his eyes again. "Why not?"

"Because what if I'm wrong? That would be very embarrassing."

He chuckled and nuzzled her neck. His voice was muffled, but she heard him say, "You're not wrong."

The admission filled her chest and spread out into the rest of her body. She hugged him to her tightly, and they stayed like that for a couple of minutes.

When she finally started shifting beneath him, she felt his erection through his pants jutting against her thigh. She parted her legs to make room for his body and loosened her arms so he could prop himself back up above her.

They smiled at each other rather stupidly for a few seconds before he kissed her again, more intentionally this time. It wasn't long before it deepened into more than kissing. She was rocking up into him shamelessly when he unexpectedly flipped them over so that she was on top of him.

It was skillfully done. She didn't have a chance to feel awkward or off-balance. She squealed in surprise when he moved them, but before the squeal was finished, she was already sprawled out on top of him.

"Feeling lazy this morning?" she asked, kissing a line down his neck toward his chest because it was laid out beneath her so irresistibly.

"Yep. Thought you could do most of the work."

"That's not very gentlemanly."

"Hey, whoever claimed I was a gentleman? I'm a dick,

remember. You said so yourself. Plus I've only had a few hours of sleep."

She was using her lips to tease his nipples in turn. "Poor victimized Lincoln. Forced to have sex at eight thirty on a Saturday morning."

His hands were running up and down her back and bottom with delicious entitlement. "It's a burden. My wife is a real taskmaster."

"Your wife is the one doing all the work here, so what exactly are you complaining about?"

He chuckled and took her face in his hands, holding it for a moment before letting his palms slide down to her neck. "I'm not complaining about a thing. My wife is the best thing to ever happen to me."

Her heart leaped. Her blood leaped. Everything inside her leaped. Parting her lips slightly, she searched his face. She saw a familiar dry humor there as if he were laughing at himself a little. Did that mean he didn't mean what he said?

He chuckled as he lowered his hands to her hips. "You think this marriage hasn't been good to me? You think finding sex this good is easy?"

Oh. That was what he was talking about.

She quickly convinced herself there was nothing to be disappointed about, so she was able to reply in a matching teasing tone. "I thought you were some sort of sex god who had sex like this all the time."

"Not all the time." He pulled her back down into a kiss and murmured against her lips. "Almost never."

She smiled since that was nice to hear. And it was safer than that uproar of emotion she'd almost indulged. The kiss deepened until they were both urgent and grinding against each other.

They broke the kiss so he could pull her gown off over her head. Then he took her breasts in his hands and fondled them until she was arching back and moaning uninhibitedly.

When he finally dropped his hands, she was so aroused she couldn't wait any longer. She lifted up so she could tug down his pants. He raised his hips to help her, and it didn't take long for her to yank them over his feet and drop them onto the floor.

She took his full erection in her hands and stroked the length of him until he couldn't keep his hips still. His hot green eyes were moving hungrily between her face and bare breasts as she caressed him. She massaged his balls and then lowered her face to his groin, licking a line up the underside of his shaft before taking him full in her mouth.

He choked on an exclamation and closed his eyes, tossing his head a couple of times in naked pleasure.

It was hard not to let that go to her head.

She sucked him off for a minute, but she was too aroused to take him all the way to orgasm at the moment. Letting him slip from her mouth, she rearranged her body so she was astride him.

He opened his eyes and moved a hand down to hold himself in position as she sheathed him with her body.

They'd stopped using condoms earlier in the week because they were both healthy, they weren't sleeping with anyone else, and she was on birth control.

"Oh fuck, Summer," he breathed thickly. His fingers were gripping the soft flesh of her ass. "Oh fuck."

She adjusted positions, trying to find the angle that felt ʟ best and made it easiest for her to move. She wasn't normally an on-top person, but Lincoln made every position easy and sexy. She had no idea how he did it. But any position that made his face look like *that* was something she wanted to try.

When she got comfortable, she started to lever up with her hips so she could ride him. She moved slow and steady at first, enjoying the stimulation and the look in Lincoln's eyes as he watched her move above him. He would sometimes play with her nipples. And sometimes rub her clit. And sometimes hold on to her neck with a possessive touch that was incredibly sexy.

When an orgasm tightened inside her, she picked up her speed, bouncing over him urgently so her breasts shook and thighs burned. She knew she was making a lot of embarrassing sounds of effort and pleasure, but she didn't even care.

She needed this. *Needed* it. And she was almost there.

"That's right, baby," Lincoln muttered, his eyes still devouring her. "Fuck me hard. Take it all. Don't hold anything back."

She wasn't holding anything back, and she'd never known she was capable of it before. She choked and sobbed out her pleasure as the climax finally peaked. She shook through the spasms, and Lincoln gave a muffled shout as her inner walls clamped down around him.

She was panting and grinning like a fool, enjoying the shudders of her orgasm, when Lincoln flipped them back over. He lifted one of her knees and pushed it up toward her shoulder before he started to fuck her the way she'd been fucking him. Just as hard and fast and vigorous. Just as unin-hibitedly.

She moaned because it felt so good. The rough friction inside her. The sight of Lincoln's damp, ardent face above her. The rawness of what they were doing together. She wasn't expecting to come again, but she did, crying out as the plea-sure rose up unexpectedly.

Then he was coming too with a loud bellow, his features twisting dramatically in a way that showed palpably how good he was feeling.

He collapsed on top of her when he'd ridden out the last of his spasms, ducking his head in the crook of her neck and gasping for air.

She held on to him with her arms and her legs. She wasn't about to let him go.

"You're incredible, baby," he mumbled against her throat.

She giggled. She couldn't help it. "You too." She stroked his messy hair. It was thick and soft and felt so good against her palms. "Of course now I'm exhausted, and we haven't even gotten out of bed yet."

"Well, there's no hurry, is there? It's Saturday morning. Do you have any plans today?" He lifted his head.

She smiled at him rather sappily. "I've got no plans at all today."

"Good." He rolled them over onto their sides so he could wrap his arms around her. "So let's stay in bed as long as we can."

She had no objections to that plan, but she was a bit worried at how she was feeling. Way too soft. Way too posses-sive. Way too much like their relationship could be some-thing other than it was.

And so far, despite some fond looks and sweet comments, the only specific things said about their relationship was that what they had was nothing but sex.

That was fine. She wasn't going to turn down something so good.

But she also didn't want to come out of this marriage, yearning for a man she couldn't have.

So, with a bone-deep instinct of self-preservation, she pulled herself out of his embrace. "I've got to clean up a bit before we go back to sleep. I'm all spermy." She found her gown and pulled it over her head before she stood up.

"Spermy?" He rolled over with a look of mock indignation. "You're calling it spermy?"

"Well? What else do you want me to call it? That you've graciously endowed me with your precious seed?"

He laughed warmly, his eyes caressing her even though her cheeks were blazing hot, her hair was a mess, and her gown was wrinkled and still hiked up on her hips. "I think we can do better than *spermy*."

Despite her attempt at emotional distance, she giggled at that. "You work on a better term while I go and clean up from all the sperminess."

She heard him chuckling from the bed as she made her way to the bathroom. She stayed in there longer than she needed.

Emotional distance was getting harder and harder.

∽

THE FOLLOWING AFTERNOON, Summer found Carter in the media room. That was what they called the mansion's windowless room with the huge TV.

He was watching a sports network, but a quick glance proved it was just commentary and not the exciting part of a game, so she came in and flopped down beside him.

She'd seen him fairly regularly since they were living in the same house, but it felt like she hadn't really talked to him all week.

She missed him.

He didn't feel as much like her best friend anymore, and she wanted that to change.

Change back to what it used to be.

He glanced over at her with raised eyebrows.

"Just wanted to hang out," she explained to his unspoken question. "I'm bored."

"You're never bored."

He was right. She wasn't the kind of person who ever got bored. She was always able to find something to do to amuse herself—even if it was just reading or binge-watching TV. "Well, I'm restless or something, and I wanted to hang out with you. Is something wrong with that?"

"No. You just don't do it as much anymore." He didn't look angry or bitter or even sad. Just vaguely resigned.

"Well, whose fault is that? You're the one who withdrew, Carter. Don't act like I'm the one who's done it."

For a moment she thought he might get annoyed and just leave, but he didn't. He slumped back against the couch and muttered, "Yeah. I guess. I'm sorry."

"Do you want to talk about it?"

"What's to talk about? Something has changed. You know

it has."

"Yes, but why can't it change back? If you'd just let me know what's been bothering you, I'm sure we can deal with it. We've always dealt with stuff before."

He wrapped an arm around her shoulders and pulled her over so she was leaning against him. It was an affectionate, companionable gesture that made her throat ache.

She snuggled against him happily. "So what is it?" she asked. "What's been bothering you, Carter? I miss you."

"I miss you too," he murmured, nuzzling her hair in a way that surprised her. It was like he was smelling her hair.

She tilted her face up to check his expression, but she didn't get the chance. A sound from the doorway surprised them.

Lincoln was standing in the doorway, watching them. He was wearing his running clothes, and he'd obviously just finished his run. It was in the forties outside, but he was sweating and windblown. He looked strange. Stiff. Weirdly frozen.

Summer's stomach twisted, although she didn't know why. "Hey. Did you have a good run?"

"Yeah. It was fine." He sounded just as strange as he looked.

Summer wanted to pull away from Carter—out of his arm—but there was no reason for her to feel that way. She'd been friends with Carter a lot longer than she'd been anything to Lincoln, and she wasn't going to hurt his feelings by suddenly withdrawing. "I guess you've got to go into work soon." She was trying to sound as natural as possible. At least she was trying, which was more than either of the men were doing.

"Yeah. I do." He waited for another several seconds, staring as if he were expecting something.

She didn't know what to do, so she didn't do anything.

He turned around and left.

When he was well away from the room, Summer said softly, "Well, that was weird."

"No, it wasn't." It was the first thing Carter had said since Lincoln appeared.

"What do you mean it wasn't weird? Didn't you see him?"

"Of course I saw him. I'm just saying it wasn't weird. Perfectly natural, really."

"What does that mean?" She gazed up at Carter with wide eyes, both confused and wary about what he was about to say.

"You can't be that blind, Summer. He didn't like seeing us sitting this way."

"What? Why would he care—?"

"He's into you, Summer. You've got to see it too. He's *into* you."

Ridiculously, her heart burst into excited flutters. The feeling spread up into her throat and then up far enough to warm her cheeks. "He's not—"

"Yes, he is. He's not even trying to hide it. He's never been one to keep his feelings to himself. He's into you. Don't tell me he hasn't tried to do something about it. It's not like him to hold back."

She gulped, trying to figure out what to say. "It's... it's not like that between us."

"If that's true, then it's because of you and not because of him. He's definitely into you. If you want to know what's come between us, all you need to do is look in his direction."

Summer straightened up. "That's not fair, Carter. Lincoln has done nothing but try to help you. I know things are strained between you from the past, but he hasn't done anything wrong since your father's will was read. Everything he's doing is to help you—because you asked him to. You can't blame him."

Carter leaned his head back and closed his eyes. "I know. It would be nice to blame him, but I can't. I'm the one to blame. I brought this on myself."

"What did you bring on yourself, Carter? Please talk to me. Everything is going like you planned it, isn't it?"

"No. Not at all."

"What is it? What's wrong?" She reached over to touch his sleeve.

He opened his eyes, and she thought he was going to admit it at last. But once again, he pulled whatever it was back. "It's fine, Summer. It's all fine. Lincoln is doing what he said he would with the company. He keeps trying to give me advice when he doesn't know what he's talking about, but he's not pushing his way. It's all fine."

"What advice?"

"Oh, just stuff about our business strategy after the acquisition goes through. He thinks I'm being too aggressive, and he won't shut up about it."

"What does he want to do instead?"

"He wants to move more slowly. Test the market before we redo all the properties."

She replied slowly, carefully, "Well, that doesn't sound like a terrible idea."

"It's not a terrible idea, but it's not the best idea. I'm the one who's poured himself into this company for the past decade. He hasn't done a thing. Just gotten the whole thing dropped into his lap last month. I think I might know a little more than him about our business and the hotel market."

He sounded so hurt that she stroked his shoulder and arm. "Of course you do. I didn't mean to question you. I just meant that Lincoln is probably trying to help. He's trying to be involved. That's not a bad thing, is it?"

"I guess. I'd feel better about it if I thought he was doing it because he cared about me."

"Of course he cares about you. Why else would he be helping this way?"

Carter gave her a significant look.

"Oh, come on now, Carter. Don't take it too far. He's never even mentioned any of this to me. He's not doing it because he's trying to impress me or something."

"I don't think that's what he's doing."

"Then what?"

Carter's brown eyes were strained and sad. "He's doing it because he's trying to be better. *Do* better. And I guarantee this urge to better himself is not because of me."

Summer's cheeks burned even more. She raised her hand to her chest because the flutters were completely out of control. "I... I don't think it's..."

"Well, you're wrong." He shook his head and muttered, almost to himself, "It's just like him. To come along and get involved at exactly the worst time."

"Why is it the worst time?"

Carter didn't answer. He wasn't like Lincoln. He always kept his deepest feelings to himself.

THIRTY MINUTES LATER, Summer wandered upstairs to her room since Carter had gotten involved in the sports show and obviously wasn't in the mood for talking anymore.

She walked over to the door that connected to Lincoln's room. It was halfway open. They never shut it anymore.

Summer felt jittery after what Carter had said about Lincoln. She couldn't help but wonder if he was right.

She tapped on the door and called out, "Lincoln?"

"Yeah." His voice came from his closet.

She stepped into the room as he emerged wearing black trousers and carrying a long-sleeved gray shirt. He pulled it over his head as she watched.

"What's up?" he asked, arching his dark eyebrows.

"Just checking on you." The words sounded lame to her own ears, but she didn't know what else to say.

"Why do I need to be checked on?" Then, defying his intentionally casual tone, he added, "You and Carter looked very cozy down there."

"I was trying to be his friend. Something's wrong with him, and he still won't say what it is."

"I'm beginning to suspect." He sounded cool. A lot cooler than he'd been with her in a long time.

"What do you suspect?"

"It's not really my thing to say." He opened a drawer and pulled out a pair of black socks, sitting down on the edge of the bed to pull them on.

She went to sit next to him. "Why are you acting like this, Lincoln? I thought... I thought things were going well with us."

He slanted her a look that was searching, urgent. She didn't understand it.

"Weren't they?" she asked hoarsely. "Going well?"

"I thought so."

"So what's the matter? Aren't I allowed to have this thing with you and also be Carter's friend?"

The tension suddenly blew out of him like a popped balloon. He made a throaty sound and pulled her into a hug, right there as they sat on the edge of the bed. "Of course you are, baby."

She hugged him back, more relieved than she should have been. She mumbled against his shoulder, "So then what's the problem?"

"There is no problem. Just for a minute it looked like you might want to have a *thing* with Carter too, and I wouldn't be okay with that."

She pulled back and stared at him in astonishment. "You're not serious?"

"About what?"

"Carter is my friend. Just my friend."

"And not too long ago you wanted him for something more."

"But that was before. I told you. I don't feel that way anymore. I've long since outgrown it. I'm not going back." She was telling him the truth as openly as she knew how to do. It made her scared and vulnerable, but it felt important to do so. "Don't you believe me?"

There was a long moment as he scanned her face like he was looking desperately for the truth of her words. Then he nodded and kissed her hard and brief. "Yes. I believe you."

Relaxing, she leaned against him. He kept his arms around her but more loosely this time.

"Carter suspects," she said after a minute.

"What does he suspect?"

"About us. Well, actually, he suspects about you. He thinks you're into me."

He nuzzled her neck. It was the sweetest thing. "Well, he's not wrong."

"Should we tell him? I'm starting to feel kind of guilty about hiding this thing from him."

"What would you tell him?"

She hesitated. "I don't even know."

"If you don't know what you'd tell him, it's probably best to wait until you do. But I'll leave it with you."

"So you don't want to tell him?"

"I don't know. I'm just not sure it's worth hurting him if this thing is only going to last as long as our marriage."

She straightened up, his words slicing through her chest like a blade. "Is it?"

"Is what?"

"Is it going to end with our marriage?"

They stared at each other for a long time, tension palpable—shuddering in the air between them. Then Lincoln finally shook his head. "I don't know, Summer. I don't know any more than you do."

She nodded, relieved that they'd at least gotten the unspoken questions out in the open. They didn't have to have all the answers right now. At least they seemed to be on the same page. "Okay. Then let's not tell him yet. Not until we know this is... something."

He nodded.

To change the subject, Summer said, "Carter said you'd been talking to him some about the business."

"He probably didn't say it so politely. Did he say I was interfering? Getting on his nerves?"

"Something like that."

He sighed as he pulled on his shoes. "I know I'm no expert, but it makes more sense to move slowly. He's going to blow all your money in no time and end up in the red again."

"Maybe. But isn't it possible he knows what he's doing? He's been doing this for a long time now."

Lincoln's expression changed. Hardened slightly. "And I haven't? So I don't know what I'm talking about? Now you sound like him."

"I'm not criticizing. I'm just trying to see both sides."

"But you're not really. You're seeing his side." He stood up, sounding and looking bitter in a way she hadn't seen in a really long time. "Honestly, I'm not sure why I expected anything else."

"Lincoln!" The word came out as almost a sob. "It's not like—"

"It's exactly like that, and I'm an idiot for hoping for anything different." His mouth set in something resembling a sneer. "Story of my life."

"Stop it." She stood up and hurried toward him, reaching out to take his arm. "Stop being like that. If you'd just talk about—"

"There's nothing to talk about. I understand perfectly. And I've got to go to work." He pulled out of her grip and started to leave the room.

"Lincoln, wait!"

He didn't wait. He kept striding away from her until he was out of sight.

She stood and stared at his retreating back for a minute

until she couldn't stand it anymore. This wasn't like the Lincoln she'd come to know. This was like the old Lincoln—the one she'd thought was gone for good.

She ran after him, down the hall and then the stairs. She made it to the landing just as he was opening the door that led to the large garage. "Lincoln, wait! Don't just leave!"

He did leave. He ignored her. And he was out the door before she could stop him.

She stared at the closed door for a long time until she realized there was someone else in the hall.

Carter. Watching her quietly.

She didn't understand his expression at all.

He reached out a hand toward her in invitation.

She went over to take it, letting him lead her back to the media room to spend the evening with him.

SUMMER ENDED up having a decent evening, although she couldn't completely rid her mind of the argument with Lincoln. When she went to bed, she was upset about it all over again, and she couldn't go to sleep.

He was working. He wouldn't be back until late. She needed to go to sleep and deal with it in the morning.

But she couldn't sleep. The distraction that Carter had provided was completely gone now, and all she could do was toss and turn and brood about Lincoln.

It was almost two when she heard his bedroom door open and saw light from the hallway. The connecting door was wide open.

She lay stiffly in bed and waited to see if he'd come see

her. He usually did even if it was just to give her a sleepy kiss.

Tonight he didn't come. She heard him walk to the bathroom. Heard the door click. Heard the faint sound of the toilet. Then the shower. He wasn't in there long. Just taking a quick shower to wash off hours spent in the bar. A few more minutes passed, during which she imagined he was brushing his teeth and getting ready for bed.

It was only then, after that, she saw his figure silhouetted in the doorway. He was standing there, looking in on her. She waited. Didn't move.

He didn't say anything.

After a few minutes, he turned around and went to his own bed.

And that was the last straw. She rolled out of bed and stomped across the room and into his.

"Summer?" he asked softly. He'd climbed under the covers and raised his upper body halfway when he realized she was there. "What are you doing?"

"Asshole," she gritted out, crawling into his bed beside him.

"I thought you were asleep."

"I wasn't asleep. And if you'd bothered to come closer, you would have known it. The least you could do after acting like a jerk is apologize."

Incongruously, it sounded like he was smiling in the dark. "I am sorry. I'm really sorry. I was an asshole. I never should have put you in the position of choosing between me and your best friend."

"No. You shouldn't. But that wasn't the big deal. The big deal was walking out before we even talked about it. In what world is that appropriate behavior?"

"In no world. It's appropriate behavior in no world. But I'm a dick, remember? That's the kind of thing I've always done." He'd turned on his side to face her, but he wasn't touching her. "So there's no reason for you to forgive me."

"Well, I do," she grumbled.

"What?"

"I do. Forgive you. If you're really sorry and you promise to work on not doing it again. I forgive you."

"Baby?" The question was faint, hoarse.

"I forgive you."

"Why?"

"Because I get it. It's a really hard situation. For you as much as me. I get it. Just don't walk out in the middle of a fight again."

He made a throaty sound and pulled her against him, wrapping his arms around her. "Okay. I won't. I'm sorry."

She burrowed against his warm body, smelling soap and a faint trace of whiskey and Lincoln. "Good."

He brushed a few kisses into her hair. "I thought I'd lost you. I thought that was it for us."

"That's because you're stupid. Haven't you ever been in a relationship before?"

"A real one? No. I haven't."

"Oh. I guess that explains the stupidity." She was smiling too now. Rather foolishly. She didn't care. She hugged him to her. "Now, I'm tired, and I have to go to work tomorrow, so I'm going to go to sleep."

He kissed her again. Her neck this time. His arms loosened just enough for her to get comfortable. "Sounds good to me."

8

ON THURSDAY OF THAT WEEK, SUMMER WENT OUT WITH HER friends. She hadn't spent much time with them for the past month since she'd been busy with work, Carter, and Lincoln, so she was excited to get together with them and have some girl time.

She'd had a lot of man time recently, and frankly she needed the break.

They got together after work and had dinner at their favorite pasta place. No one was ready to go home afterward, so they decided to go to Milhouse for an after-dinner drink.

Milhouse was the bar where Lincoln worked.

Summer made a feeble attempt to suggest a different place, but Milhouse was the best bar in Green Valley. Not only were the drinks the best, but it was more comfortable and not as loud as the one trendy club in town.

So they ended up at Milhouse, even though Lincoln was working behind the bar tonight.

Summer wasn't sure why she was so nervous about going, but she was.

Only Nona, her best female friend, knew the real reason for her marriage to Lincoln. To everyone else she'd used the same cover story they were sharing with the rest of the town. Summer was realistic about the way gossip worked. If she told too many people the truth, it would eventually get around—embarrassing all of them and possibly threatening the legitimacy of her investment in Wilson Hotels.

She wasn't going to risk it, no matter how bad she felt about lying to some of her friends.

It wouldn't last for long.

Soon the acquisition would have gone through officially, and she and Lincoln could get a divorce.

She tried to feel relieved by that eventuality, but mostly it made her feel sick.

The first thing she saw when she came into the bar with her friends was Lincoln, looking sleek and modern and ridiculously attractive as he chatted with a couple of women as he shook up a drink.

The women were flirting. That much was obvious in the time it took them to snag a small round table in a corner before another group grabbed it. The women Lincoln was talking to were definitely liking him.

And why wouldn't they? Who wouldn't? He was gorgeous and sexy and charming and could make anyone laugh.

This was his job, and Summer wasn't going to be silly about it.

He could talk to anyone he wanted—just like her.

Nona collected the drink orders and then dragged Summer up to the bar with her, whispering, "It will look very suspicious if you don't even say hi to your husband."

"He's busy."

"He's not too busy to say hi to his wife."

Summer grumbled some more—merely out of principle —but she knew her friend was right. If people were going to believe they had a regular marriage, it wouldn't make sense for her not to greet him.

And the truth was she wanted to greet him. She just felt awkward and self-conscious about it since it felt like all her friends would be watching.

Lincoln had spotted her before she started walking up to the bar. He said something to the two women as he finished pouring their drinks, and then he made a beeline for the other side of the bar where Summer and Nona were approaching.

He was grinning as he reached them, and he leaned all the way over the bar so he could give her a quick kiss on the lips. "Hey. I didn't know you were stopping by."

"That's because I didn't know myself." Summer was blushing, which was silly. But it felt like she and Lincoln were the center of attention. Like everyone was checking them out. Watching how they acted and speculating about their relationship.

She didn't like to be the center of attention. She never had.

But the truth was she wanted everyone to know that she and Lincoln were together for real. It was a silly, almost immature instinct, but it felt like she was suddenly sexy and desirable in a way she'd never felt before, and she wanted the rest of the world to realize it too.

"What can I get you all?" He glanced back at the table where their friends were waiting. "You want that daiquiri you like?"

She nodded. "The others want cosmos except for Nona."

Lincoln twitched his eyebrows at Nona. "Whiskey sour?"

"Yep." Nona slanted Summer a smile. "He's good."

"He's good at a lot of things." The most ridiculous thing was the words just came out. She didn't even say it for her pose as a newlywed.

Lincoln's eyes warmed. He made a summoning gesture with his hand, and Summer stood on tiptoes and leaned over to meet him halfway across the bar to kiss him again. This one wasn't quite so quick.

She was flushed hot when she pulled away. She turned toward Nona as Lincoln went to work on the drinks.

Nona was giving her a significant, knowing stare.

"What?" Summer demanded.

"You know what."

"I don't know anything."

"Oh my goodness. Yes, you do. There's no way that's all an act. You were never a very good actor."

Summer leaned over to murmur, "You know what this marriage is about."

"I know what it's supposed to be about, but it looks like a lot more than that to me. Don't lie to me."

"I'm not going to lie to you. Something is going on. But neither one of us knows what it is yet, so don't push."

"Okay." Nona didn't look worried or wary. In fact, she looked thrilled. "But as soon as you know, you have to tell me everything."

"I will. I always do."

When their drinks were done, Summer and Nona carried them back over to where their friends were waiting. They drank and chatted and had a really good time.

After about an hour, Summer was surprised when someone came up beside her and edged her over on her chair. She jerked in surprise before she realized it was Lincoln.

"What are you doing?" she asked, giggling as he made room for himself on the seat by the simple expedience of moving her onto his lap.

"I'm on my break, and it looks like y'all are having fun over here."

"We were. But it was girl fun." She rubbed her cheek against his shoulder. "No one said you were invited."

The others objected vehemently when Lincoln teased about leaving since he wasn't wanted. Then he entertained them with a couple of stories about wild customers he'd served that week.

Summer laughed with the others. And she loved the feel of his arm around her waist.

It felt like they were really together, and she wanted it that way.

Maybe they could be. Maybe this wasn't just about sex and convenience and availability.

Maybe there was something deep here.

Something that could last.

At the moment, she couldn't think of a good reason why it wasn't a possibility.

BECAUSE SHE WAS out for so long, she got to bed much later than usual.

She should have been tired, but she felt wired instead.

Like something really good was going to happen soon, and she could hardly wait for it.

Maybe there was no good reason for it, but after the way they'd talked after their argument and then the way Lincoln had acted with her at the bar, she thought that there might be reason for hope.

She wasn't normally a clueless person. And there were enough clues now for her to put together a reasoned conclusion.

Maybe Lincoln really did have feelings for her.

The same kind of feelings she had for him.

She wanted to *know*. She didn't want to go through her days on emotional pins and needles. She wanted to be able to let go of her heart. To make plans for the future.

She wanted to know if Lincoln might be part of her future.

It was still early. She wasn't going to expect too much too soon. She didn't need any guarantees right now. She just needed to know it was a real beginning and not just great sex to pass the time.

So she got into her own bed—even though she really wanted to sleep in Lincoln's—and she tried to sleep for hours. One came and went. Then two. Then three. Lincoln should be home by now, but he wasn't.

He wasn't—she knew for sure—out with another woman. But she didn't know where he was. She eventually fell into a restless sleep and woke to her alarm at the normal time of six thirty. Her head was fuzzy and eyes heavy, but it was Friday, so she just needed to make it through to the weekend.

She stumbled into the shower and she was halfway through lathering up her hair when she remembered Lincoln hadn't come home before she'd fallen asleep last night. She rushed through the rest of her shower and threw on a bathrobe to go check out his room.

She wasn't going to wake him up. She just needed to see him sleeping, and then she'd quiz him about his unusual hours later.

Her stomach dropped when she realized he wasn't there. His bed hadn't been slept in. He'd never come home.

Maybe she was hopelessly naive, but she still didn't believe he'd spent the night with another woman. It never even occurred to her as a possibility.

The first and only conclusion her mind leaped to was that something bad had happened.

Something had happened to Lincoln.

She ran back to her bedroom to grab her phone and hit his number with trembling fingers. She held her breath as it rang.

She almost choked on her relief when his voice finally answered. "Hey. Good morning." He sounded tired but generally healthy.

"Good morning! You're telling me good morning! Where the hell are you?"

"I'm walking through the front door right now." He spoke slowly, sounding a little confused. "What's the matter?"

"What's the matter? You didn't come home last night. I woke up, and you weren't here. I thought something had happened. I was..." She sat on her bed in her wet hair and bathrobe, realizing she might have overreacted a little bit.

"You were what?" He was slightly breathless now, like he was running.

He'd definitely been running because he was suddenly in

the doorway of her room, still dressed in the clothes he'd worn to work last night and looking tense and questioning.

She kept the phone at her ear—because she was that befuddled—and she stared back at him.

"You were what?" he asked again, coming into the room and closing the door behind him.

"I was scared," she admitted in a silly stage whisper.

His face was washed with a series of transparent emotions. Surprise. Hope. Joy. Something like awe. "You were scared?"

She disconnected the call and set her phone on the bed beside her. "Of course I was scared. Why wouldn't I be scared? You were supposed to be home, and you weren't. Where were you?"

He sat beside her, reaching over to take her hand from her lap. "Shit, your hands are cold and still shaking. You *were* scared."

"I told you I was. What happened?"

"We had a crisis at the bar. A pipe burst and the kitchen flooded. It was a mess. I had to stay and help clean up and then wait for the plumber. I'm sorry you were scared." He'd reached for her other hand too, and he was rubbing them with his big, warm ones.

His gentle tone and touch relaxed the tension in her body and chest. "Was there a lot of damage?"

"Some, but nothing too expensive, I hope. It was mostly just cleaning up the water." He dropped one of her hands so he could wrap an arm around her back. "It never occurred to me that anyone would worry about me."

"Well, I would. I did." She leaned her head against his

chest as he pulled her closer. "You should have let me know where you were."

"Okay." He sounded too thick. Almost gravelly. "From now on, I will."

They stayed like that for a long time—holding hands on his lap as she leaned against him, his arm wrapped tightly around her.

Her heart had burst into those same flutters she'd been feeling for a while now, but they were so strong and so chaotic she could barely contain them in her chest.

She'd done this all her life—kept her feelings to herself, safely contained by her reserve, until they got strong like this. Then they burst out whether she wanted them or not, often in the least strategic ways.

They burst out now. "This is... this is... more than sex. Between us, I mean." She gulped and pulled away so she could see his face. "Isn't it?"

He finally let go of her hand so he could hold the side of her neck. "It is on my side. I didn't know about you."

She made a sound halfway between a sob and a giggle. "It is on my side too."

"Yeah?"

"Yeah."

His expression softened. Warmed with the most delicious sort of heat. So much more than lust. "Thank God, baby. I've been dying over this for weeks now, not wanting to pressure you or move too soon."

"It's not too soon." She couldn't seem to stop smiling.

He was starting to smile too. He leaned over to kiss her, still holding on to her neck, but both of them couldn't stop smiling enough to concentrate, so it was kind of clumsy. They eventually settled with hugging, both of them shaking with soft laughter instead.

It was only then that Summer caught a glimpse of the clock. "Shit. I've got to dry my hair this morning, and it takes forever."

Lincoln was grinning fully. Nothing held back. She'd never seen him look like that before. He gave her a quick kiss as he stood up. "You go do that. I'm hot and sweating and still damp from floodwater. I'm going to take a shower."

"Okay. Good plan." She'd much rather stay where they were and keep hugging, but work wasn't going to wait just because she was suddenly blissfully happy.

Lincoln walked to the door that connected their rooms, but he turned back before he went through. "Don't go to work while I'm in there."

She laughed. "Don't worry. Unless you're planning to take a twenty-five-minute shower, I'll still be working on my hair."

Summer's daily routine was fairly low maintenance, but on days when she washed her hair, she always took the time to blow it out straight since she liked it smooth and shiny. Since her hair was thick and long, it took a long time to do.

She set to work on the job with her brush and hair dryer. And for once, the tedious task was punctuated with smiles and giggles. Twice she stopped to hug herself.

She really couldn't help it.

When Lincoln reappeared, he was dressed for bed in his pajama pants. She was working on the last section of her hair, but she gave his bare chest and low-slung pants an exaggerated leer that made him chuckle.

After she'd turned off the dryer and brushed out her hair, he came over and pulled her into a kiss. Maybe it was supposed to be a quick kiss to say goodbye for the morning, but it got deep very quickly. His body felt so good—so hard and warm and masculine—and what she could sense of his heart—just as warm, just as big, which he tried so much to hide from the world—felt even better.

She was all over him, rubbing up against him and dragging her fingers down his bare back. When she discovered he was already hard, she ground herself against the bulge, making both of them groan.

"Do you have time for something before work?" he mumbled, kissing a line down her neck before he returned to her mouth.

She managed to focus on the bedside clock enough to make out the time. "Maybe. If we're really quick."

"I can be quick."

"That hasn't been my experience with you in bed."

"Well, I haven't faced a time challenge in the past, but I guarantee you I'll be up for it."

"All right. No dillydallying."

"Got it. No dillydallying. We won't even use the bed."

"How exactly are you planning to fuck me without the bed?"

"Are you doubting my ingenuity? There are plenty of empty walls." He backed her all the way to the wall that faced the hallway where there was nothing but a dresser and a small console table near the door.

"You're really thinking about wall sex? After fighting flood waters all night?"

He laughed, his fond green eyes resting on her face like a caress. "That's a good point." He glanced around. "I could use a little help." He moved them over a few feet to the console table and propped her up on it.

She squealed. "I'm not sure this table is made to the hold the weight of a person."

He wiggled the table with her on top of it, making her squeal again. "It will do just fine. I have faith in it."

She was giggling helplessly when he kissed her again. When his hands got busy under the bathrobe she still wore, arousal started to grow inside her, mingling with her amusement and the giddy emotion that hadn't yet dimmed.

She was full of everything she felt—almost too full—as he kissed her hungrily and tweaked her breasts at the same time. When the pleasure became almost torturous, he moved his hands downward. His wandering fingers discovered that she was already wet and ready for him, but instead of getting going on the main event, he penetrated her with two fingers and started to pump them.

She gasped and whimpered and clung to him desperately, feeling off-balance on the narrow table. She came absurdly fast, mewing out the pleasure against his mouth, but then she had the sense to remind him, "No more foreplay. I know you're ambitious, but we're in a time crunch here."

He grumbled unconvincingly as he pulled out his erection and positioned himself at her entrance. Her hair and her open robe were falling over both of them as he pushed in.

Then he found her lips again as he started to rock his hips. He was holding her up, filling her up. For the moment he was everything.

And it was exactly what she wanted him to be.

"Oh fuck, baby, you're everything," he rasped against her mouth. "Everything. To me. Everything."

It was like he read her mind.

She arched and gasped and couldn't hold back her mews of pleasure—emotional as much as physical. "Please. Please don't stop."

"I won't. Ever." His speed was accelerating. He didn't have nearly as much control this morning as he normally did, and it was thrilling to realize it might be because he was just as overwhelmed as emotion as she was. "Ever, baby. Ever."

She dug her fingernails into the back of his shoulders as an orgasm started to crest. "Harder, Lincoln. Please. Harder."

He responded to her pleas, thrusting into her with so much vigor that they knocked the table against the wall in a loud staccato. It only made it better, wilder, rawer. The pleasure in her body and heart threatened to split her apart as she cried out with her release.

He choked back a loud exclamation as her body clamped down around him. He jerked and pushed and grunted through his final thrusts before he let go too. Just as fully as she had.

She clung to him desperately, both her arms and legs wrapped around him, when his motion finally grew still. Her body was relaxing with a delicious satisfaction, and she could feel the same in his.

He was murmuring something against her neck. She couldn't quite make out what it was.

But she wanted to hear it. She strained to hear it.

Instead, she heard a knock on her bedroom door.

Both of them froze for several seconds, like they were children caught in something naughty. Then the knock came again. "Summer?" It was Carter from out in the hall. "Is everything all right?"

"Shit!" That was Lincoln, soft and strained. He took a step back, sliding his softening penis out of her and quickly pulling up his pants. He helped her set her feet on the floor as she hurriedly closed her robe.

They stared each other for a moment, paralyzed with surprise and indecision.

When Carter knocked and called out again, Summer finally gave a helpless shrug. They had to open the door soon, or Carter would be worried and might just walk in.

Lincoln went to open the door. Summer followed a little behind him.

"Is everything all—?" Carter's worried question broke off as he got a look at them.

The scene was unmistakable. What they'd just been doing was just as clear as if Carter had caught them naked and going at it. Lincoln's pants were barely pulled up and his hair was sticking up almost on end. Summer was flushed and rumpled and trying to close her robe more securely.

After his half-finished question, Carter stared silently from one to the other. There was more than surprise on his face. There was something that looked like shocked pain—as if he'd just suffered a physical blow.

Summer felt sick. She began, "Carter..." But she had absolutely no idea what to say.

Carter's eyes finally landed on Summer, and he asked hoarsely, "What are you *doing*?"

She opened her mouth but couldn't think of anything to say.

"Now just a minute," Lincoln began, sounding subdued but also faintly annoyed.

Carter didn't give them a minute. He turned around and walked away.

"Carter, wait!" she called, starting after him. Then she stopped abruptly when she remembered the time. "Damn it. I have an eight-o'clock meeting. I can't be late." She was close to tears of worry and frustration. "This is terrible. Poor Carter. He shouldn't have found out that way."

"I'll talk to him," Lincoln said, hiking up his pants and running a hand through his wildly disordered hair. "You go ahead and get dressed. I'll talk to him."

"But—"

"He's my brother, baby. It needs to be me."

She nodded, hugging her arms to her chest.

He stepped over to give her a soft kiss, running a hand lightly down the length of her hair. "I'll take care of it," he murmured. "It's going to be okay."

She didn't believe it, but it made her feel better anyway.

9

SUMMER MANAGED TO GET DRESSED AND GET INTO WORK IN time for her meeting, but she was flustered and distracted, and it wasn't her finest hour.

As soon as her meeting was over, she texted Lincoln. *How's Carter?*

He didn't answer right away, and she had to get through a twenty-five-minute phone call before she was able to check her phone again.

He still hadn't answered.

Everything all right?

When five minutes had passed and there was still no reply, she called him instead. He hadn't yet gotten any sleep after a long night of work, but he wouldn't have gone to bed without letting her know what was happening. The phone rang several times before the voice mail picked up.

Lincoln never checked his voice mail. She'd learned that weeks ago. Anyone who foolishly tried to contact him through a voice mail message was doomed to be ignored. She hung up and breathed deeply, controlling her rising panic.

This wasn't necessarily a bad thing. Lincoln had been in his pajamas. He hadn't had his phone with him when he went to talk to Carter. Maybe they were having a long talk. Maybe they were working things out.

It hadn't really been that long. She wasn't going to assume the worst. She wasn't going to fall apart.

She made herself focus on work until lunchtime, when she still hadn't heard anything.

She texted one more time. *Any updates???*

This time a response came in. *Explain when you get home.*

She stared at the words. They were strange. Too abrupt. Too vague. They didn't sound like a Lincoln who'd worked things out with his brother.

She glanced at the clock. The Wilson mansion was only eight minutes away from the Hope House offices where she worked. She had an hour for lunch, and no one would complain if she took a few extra minutes. She wasn't going to wait until five to find out what was going on with Lincoln and Carter.

She grabbed her purse and coat and headed for her car.

When she got to the house, she saw that Carter's car was gone from the garage, but Lincoln's was still parked in its regular spot. At least Lincoln was home.

Maybe he was sleeping. If he was, she would have to wake him up.

She ran up the west wing stairs and then into her own bedroom. When she saw the connecting door was open like normal, she pushed into Lincoln's room.

He was in bed, but he wasn't asleep. He sat up abruptly as she ran in. "What are you doing?" he said, rather grumpily.

"What do you think I'm doing? Tell me what the hell is going on. How's Carter?"

His face contorted briefly, as if he were processing heavy emotion, and she knew immediately that this was a bad sign. "He's Carter. Noble, frustrating, and completely clueless."

"What does that mean?" She toed off her shoes and climbed onto the bed beside him, sitting on her knees. "Lincoln, I'm going crazy here. What did Carter say?"

"He said I'm a selfish asshole who's been using you heartlessly, and I should know better." He wasn't really looking at her. He was staring down at the covers. "He said I was going to break your heart, and he'd never forgive me for it."

"What? Didn't you tell him...? Didn't you tell him how... how things are between us?" She reached out to grab his forearm, shocked when he jerked it out of her touch.

"It doesn't matter," Lincoln muttered. Whatever emotion he'd been processing had evidently been sucked back into tight control. His words were low and uninflected.

"What do you mean it doesn't matter?" Summer was close to tears. She suddenly knew—*knew*—what was about to happen, and she had no idea if she was capable of stopping it. "Lincoln, you... you care about me. And I feel the same way. I know it might be kind of hard for Carter to get used to it, but I'm sure—"

"Listen to me, Summer." Lincoln was meeting her eyes at last, his gaze harder than she'd ever seen it. And aching at the same time. "It doesn't matter. It can't matter. It's never going to work between us."

"W-what?" She raised her hand to cover her mouth, a painful shuddering starting in her heart and spreading everywhere.

"It's not going to work. I'm sorry."

"You're sorry?" she choked. "You're *sorry*!" She wanted to sob, but the shock was too new. The pain was numbing her, and the tears in her eyes didn't fall. "Why are you doing this? We were... we were happy. You were happy. Just a few hours ago."

"I know I was happy." Lincoln jerked his eyes away as if he couldn't look at her face anymore. "But everything's different now."

"What's different?" Her voice was too loud, too desperate. Her vision was blurring. And Lincoln's frozen body and blank face were the worst things she could imagine seeing. "Tell me what the fuck happened. Tell me right now. You can't do this to me without giving me a good reason."

"I... can't." He wouldn't look at her. Wouldn't move.

She slapped him. Not hard. Mostly just to get his attention. She'd never seen him like this before. She'd never seen anyone. "Talk to me!"

"I am talking to you."

"No, you're not. You're not telling me anything. What did Carter say to make you do this to me?"

"I can't... I can't tell you."

"You sure as hell better tell me." She was so outraged and heartbroken she couldn't stay sitting on the bed. She stood up and glared down at him. "I'm not going to let you get away with this, Lincoln Wilson. Maybe you've always run away whenever things get too hard, but you're not going to run away from this. We have something. It's real. And I think it's going to last. You don't get to just throw it away like it's nothing."

Lincoln's tightly reined emotion was suddenly let loose.

He hauled himself out of the bed and stood in front of her. "I know it's not nothing. I *know*."

"Then why are you treating it as nothing? Why are you giving up just when it was getting good?" The reality caught up with her then, and she sobbed a few times into her hands.

"Oh shit, baby. Please don't—"

"Don't you dare call me that!" She spit the words out as she dropped her hands. "You don't get to call me that if you're going to treat me like this. I... I love you, Lincoln."

He froze for a moment, staring at her blindly.

"I love you," she repeated, more confident in the words as she spoke them. "And I'm pretty sure you love me too. So whatever is going on, we can get over it."

"We can't."

"Yes, we can. You love me. Admit it!"

He shook his head, his face contorting as if he was hurting just as much as she was. "I'm so sorry, bab—Summer. I'm so sorry. But I can't admit it. I can't say it. I can't do anything. Not anymore."

She could tell he meant it. She could tell his decision was inviolable. "Why not? Tell me why! Why, Lincoln? Why?"

Her repeated demands finally broke the last thread of his control. He burst out with the answer. "Because Carter wants you too!"

That was the last thing she ever expected to hear. It took several seconds for the words to even register. Then she blinked several times, all her anger and urgency blown out in a rush. "Wh-what?"

He cleared his throat and looked away. "Carter wants you too. So I can never have you."

"Wha— But— What the hell are you talking about? Carter is my friend. He's never—"

"Not until he realized he was losing you. Then he realized he feels more for you than he thought. That's why he's been such a wreck lately. That's why he's pulled away. He wants you, Summer. He loves you."

"But... but..." She rubbed her face, trying to force her brain to work. "Are you sure? This doesn't sound right."

"Of course it's not right. It's the fucking sadistic universe being vindictive. Punishing me for my life of sin. But it's true, Summer. He loves you, and he wants you the way I do. So whatever was between us can never work."

"But why not?" She was shaking again. Not with anger but with growing despair. Because this felt real. Felt final. "Even if he does feel that way, he'll get over it. I don't feel that way for him. You know I don't. I love *you*, Lincoln. And I want—"

"Stop it!" Lincoln choked the word out. His head was turned sharply to the side, as if he didn't dare to let himself look at her. "Please stop staying that. You've got to stop tempting me. I've made my decision, baby. It's not going to work between us."

Summer was crying for real now. "But why not? I know it's hard, but why can't we somehow make it work?"

"Because he's my brother!"

Summer grew still at the hoarse, desperate words. She stared at Lincoln through her tears.

"He's my brother," he repeated, softer now. "I'm so sorry. But he's my brother. And you were his long before you were ever the slightest bit mine. When I thought he didn't want you like that, I thought it would be safe to... to see if what I've wanted for so long might have a chance. But he does. And I can keep cursing a cruel universe that let him get to you first, but it will never change the fact that he did. I'll never, never do something like that to him. I might be a sinner, but I'm not going to go that far. I'm not *that* bad. I'm not *that* selfish. It doesn't matter if it breaks my heart. I'm not going to do it."

Summer started crying again. "But it's breaking my heart too."

He made a rough sound in his throat and turned his back to her. He was hurting. She could see it in the tension of his shoulders, the set of his head. He was hurting just as much as she was. But it didn't make a difference because Lincoln was the most stubborn person she'd ever met in her life. And he'd made his decision. "I'm sorry, baby. I'm sorry. But we'll have the paperwork for the acquisition finalized next week. Then we can all move on."

She sobbed. Hugged her arms to her chest and shook helplessly. When Lincoln didn't turn around, she finally ran out of the room.

She threw herself on the bed so she could cry, but she jumped back up almost immediately.

Stumbling over, she closed the connecting door between their rooms. Then she locked it with a loud click.

It felt as final as anything ever had.

SHE DIDN'T GO BACK to work that day. She called in sick, and with the way she was feeling, it wasn't even a lie. Her whole body ached. Her head pounded. And every time she thought she was going to pull it together, she started to cry again.

Lincoln left the house shortly after their conversation,

and he didn't come back. Neither did Carter. Nona came over in the evening to cheer her up, but the Wilson brothers were nowhere to be found.

Summer thought she would start to feel better after the shock of the first day, but she actually felt worse as the weekend progressed. It was like the pain in her heart was bleeding out into her body, making it ache, making it hot and cold in turn.

On Sunday she could barely make herself get out of bed. Her head was fuzzy, and she missed Lincoln. She missed Carter too. It felt like all the men she'd counted on had deserted her, and she was left there all alone with only Mrs. Wilson's occasional pleasantries.

It felt like she was an orphan all over again with nothing to her name but a ludicrous fortune she'd never done anything to deserve.

At seven o'clock in the evening, she took a long shower, hoping that would revive her. Then, since she'd barely eaten all day, she wandered down to the kitchen. She wasn't hungry, but she vaguely believed that a little food might help her feel better.

She was surprised to see Carter in the kitchen, standing in front of the open refrigerator as if he were searching blindly for something to eat.

He whirled around when she made a noise.

"Hey," she said, surprised when her voice came out as a croak.

"Are you okay?" he asked, his handsome face frowning in concern.

She stared at him in exhausted astonishment. "What do you think?"

He closed his eyes. "I'm sure you must hate me."

"I don't hate you. But it would have been nice if you hadn't been avoiding me all weekend. I thought we were friends."

"We are. Of course we are. But I didn't know how to... I didn't think you'd want to see me." His eyes were torn. Sincere. Carter-like.

Her heart clenched with an affection that was decades old. "Well, you were wrong." Her eyes burned, but the tears didn't fall. She didn't have any tears left in her.

His mouth twisted, and he took a few steps over until he could wrap an arm around her and pull her into a quick, hard hug. "I'm so sorry, Summer. I'm sorry for everything. The whole thing is my fault, and I can never make it up to you."

She sniffed and hugged him back. "It's not all your fault. You didn't do it on purpose. But it's a mess. That's for sure."

"Yeah." The refrigerator was still hanging open, and he turned back toward it. "Are you hungry?"

"Not really. But I haven't eaten all day, and I feel like I might pass out. So I should probably try something."

"There's some leftover soup in here. Chicken and rice?"

"Yeah. That sounds okay. Let's try that."

It helped to have something to do. They warmed up the soup and cut a few pieces off a baguette and split a bottle of chilled Pellegrino. They took their food to the kitchen table, and Summer was relieved to get off her feet. Her legs were shaky. She didn't know why she felt so weak and achy.

"Have you seen Lincoln at all?" Carter asked mildly, after they'd eaten a few minutes in silence.

She shook her head. "Not since the middle of the day on Friday. He worked Friday and Saturday nights, but he doesn't work tonight. I don't know where he is. He's not going to talk to me."

Carter stared down at his soup. "He said... he said he wasn't going to keep seeing you. He said it was no big deal."

Summer blinked. "Then he lied to you. He broke things off with me, but it was a very big deal. To both of us."

"Really?" Carter's eyes shot up to her face.

Frowning, she put down her spoon. She didn't have the energy to hold it up. "Carter, do you realize what was going on between us?"

"You... had a thing."

"It was more than a thing. I love him, Carter. And he loves me."

She could tell the words surprised and hurt him. He raised a hand to rub his jaw and stared at her with bleary eyes.

"Maybe Lincoln didn't make that clear to you, but we're in love. And he broke things off with me anyway. For you."

"Summer." Carter's voice broke, so he tried again. "Summer, I didn't ask him to do that. I never would have demanded something like that. You know that."

"Yes, I know that. But he thinks you... He believes that you..."

"That I love you." He said the words simply. Softly. "I do."

If Summer had been capable of crying anymore, she would have started to do so right now. "I love you too, Carter. But as a friend. Not like that. It's never been like that between us."

Carter put down the piece of bread he'd been holding and leaned forward, closer to her. "I know it's never been that way, but that's because I've been blind. I'm not asking or expecting anything from you, Summer. Not now. But I want more from you. I really do. I didn't realize it until I saw you and him together. I saw you looking at someone else like... like..."

"Like I used to look at you." She could see the truth on his face.

"And I realized what I was losing. I'm so sorry I didn't see it before, but I see it now. And I can't help but want... I'm not going to ask anything of you right now. I wouldn't do that to you. But I can't lie to you and say I don't feel the way I feel."

"But it's... it's too late."

Carter ducked his head. "Maybe it is. It doesn't change how I feel."

Summer took another spoonful of soup and made herself swallow it down. Her throat hurt. Really bad. Almost as bad as her head. She could barely hold herself up straight. She'd never known heartache could make someone feel so sick.

Carter started eating again too, and they sat in silence for a few minutes, processing what had been said. Carter almost finished his soup, and Summer only ate about a third of hers.

Finally she cleared her mind enough to say slowly, "Carter, I love him."

Carter winced like he'd been hit.

"I'm sorry if that hurts you, but it's true. He loves me too. He's trying to be good right now. He's trying to be loyal to you. But it's not fair of you to let him do it. You've got to... make things right with him so we can be happy."

"It's more complicated than that. I'm sorry. I'm not trying to be a bastard here. But it's complicated. And I love you too much to let you get into a situation that's going to hurt you. I know you don't think so right now, but he's going to hurt you. You can't trust him."

"Yes, I can! I know I can. And he's been showing you for months that you can trust him too."

Carter kept shaking his head, licking his lips. He wasn't meeting her eyes.

"You can't do this!" Summer demanded, her voice barely recognizable from its hoarseness. Every word she spoke grated on her throat. "Carter, please. It's not fair. It's not like you to do this."

"I know it's not like me, but I don't know what else to do."

"Why can't you try to trust him? Why can't you see that he's changed?"

"Because I've had a lifetime of hoping that he'd change. A *lifetime*. And every time I think he's finally changed, every time I give him a chance, every time I try to trust him, he blows it. He drops the ball. He hurts me."

Summer swayed slightly, her head pounding and her heart pounding even more. "What... what did he do to you?"

Groaning and pushing his chair back from the table, Carter said, "About five years ago, I worked on getting him involved in the business again. Dad acted like he'd given up on Lincoln, but I knew it bothered him that Lincoln had abandoned us. So I kept at him for a few months, trying to get him involved in a possible deal I was working on. For a while it worked. Lincoln came to some meetings. They really liked him. He's way better at schmoozing than I am, and he had them on our side. He convinced them to go through with the deal. It was another possible acquisition, and it would have turned our company around five years ago without having to go through all the stuff we've had to go through now. I was so happy. Lincoln was coming back to us. He was helping us. And we were finally going to save the company for Dad."

Summer was holding her head up on her arm propped on the table. It was too heavy to hold up on her own. "What happened?" she rasped.

Carter looked away. "Lincoln bailed. All he had to do was show up for one final meeting, and he blew it. He didn't show up. He was drunk off his ass with no explanation. I tried to salvage the deal, but Lincoln was the one they wanted to work with. There was nothing I could do. The deal was blown. Wilson Hotels didn't get turned around. And Dad never trusted me again."

She could barely breathe. Barely swallow over the ache in her throat.

"Summer, I'm sorry I had to tell you this. I promised him I never would, but... but you have to know. You have to see what he's like. I love him. Of course I do. But I can't trust him. He bails whenever it gets too hard, whenever it gets too real. He's going to do it to you too, and I'm not going to sit here and let it happen if there's something I can do about it. I won't. Even if I can never have you myself, I'm not going to let him hurt you like he's hurt me." He reached over and covered her hand on the table. "Do you believe me?"

She nodded, still unable to get a word out.

"The stupid thing is I still would have forgiven him. If he'd had any sort of explanation, any sort of reason for what he'd done. But he didn't. He laughed at me and said I was an idiot for thinking he could ever be anything but what he was. I've learned my lesson. It's taken years and years, but I've learned my lesson with Lincoln. He's my brother, and I'll always love him. But that doesn't mean I'll ever trust him again."

Summer sat and shook for a long time, staring down at the table. She had no idea what to say. What to do. What to think. Her head was too cloudy and her body too weak to move or say a word.

Carter squeezed her hand. "Are you okay, Summer?"

She shook her head.

"I'm really sorry. Maybe I shouldn't have told you this. But I don't know what else to do. I want to protect you even if it's from my brother."

She finally sucked in a deep breath through her nose and looked up. She licked her lips because they were bone dry. "Carter?"

"What is it? Are you all right? You're so pale."

She felt pale. She felt like the blood had completely drained from her body. "Carter, you need to let me go."

That was clearly not what he'd expected her to say. He jerked visibly. "What?"

"You need to let me go. I'm sorry it's turned out this way. I'm sorry the timing was so... so bad. So hurtful for all of us. But it is what it is. I love Lincoln. I do. I know he hurt you, and I understand why you don't trust him. But he's never hurt me like that. He's never not been there when I needed him. I love the man he is now. I trust the man he is now. I'm not expecting you to trust him, but if you love me—if you love both of us—you'll let me go even if it's hard."

"Summer, please—"

"I know it's not fair." Tears were streaming down her cheeks now even though she'd thought she'd cried herself out. "I know it's a terrible thing to ask of you. I love you so much, Carter, and I'd never hurt you for the world. It's not fair that you have to do the hardest thing and then not get anything to show for it. But sometimes that's what love... love requires of us. You need to let me go. You need to tell him that you've let me go. He's never going to let us be together if you don't. He loves you too much. He owes you too much. But I love Lincoln, Carter, and I'm never going to be happy without him. So if you mean it when you say you love me..." She sniffed and wiped her tears away.

Carter's face was damp and white. He was shaking with suppressed feeling. His hands were fisted on the table. "Summer, I can't—"

"Yes, you can. You're the best person I've ever known. You have the biggest heart. I know you can. Maybe it's wrong of me to ask this of you, but I don't know what else to do. I love him. I want to be with him. So please. Do this for me."

He took a shuddering breath. He didn't say anything.

Summer forced herself to her feet. If she didn't lie down soon, she was going to collapse. She couldn't remember ever feeling worse than she felt right now. "I'm so sorry, Carter. I do love you. You're like family to me, and you've always been. I'm sorry I can't give you what you want, but... I just can't."

She couldn't say any more. She couldn't stand anymore. She limped to the door of the kitchen and—with great effort —made it back to her room so she could fall into bed.

SHE DOZED on and off in a hot, aching haze for a couple of hours until she heard movement from the room next door.

Lincoln must be home.

She rolled off the bed and trudged to the connecting door, unlocking it and pushing it open without knocking. She didn't care if it was rude. Her whole body hurt, and her heart hurt even more.

Lincoln had been leaning over, pulling off his socks. He jerked in surprise as she walked in. His face softened as he gazed at her. "Baby, are you all right?"

"No, I'm not all right." Her throat was way too scratchy. She had no idea what was wrong with her. Even grief shouldn't have affected her like this. "Carter told me. He told me why you owed him."

Lincoln looked away with an abrupt twitch of his head. His shoulders rose and fell with a deep breath. "So I guess you hate me now."

"No, I don't hate you. I love you. Nothing has changed."

He searched her face urgently before he looked away again. "I can't, Summer. I can't. If he told you that, even after he promised not to, then he's doing everything he can to break the ties between us."

"You love me, Lincoln."

He gave a helpless shrug.

She was being slammed with waves of hot and cold. She started to sway on her feet. "Doesn't what I want matter at all?"

"Yes, it matters. But not enough for me to betray my brother."

She gave a little sob. Then her vision started to darken. She wasn't sure exactly what happened, but she could feel herself falling.

"Shit." Lincoln had closed the distance between them. He was holding her up. "What's the matter...?" His big hand was pressing her cheek, her forehead, her throat. "Fuck, baby. You're blazing hot. Why didn't you tell me you're sick?"

"I'm sick?" She stared up toward the direction of his voice, but she couldn't see anything but a blur.

"You've got a fever. You should have told me."

Before she could respond in any way, he'd swung her up into his arms and was carrying her into her bedroom.

"I'm really sick?" she mumbled, her whole body aching painfully and the cool air of the room burning her skin.

"Yes." He yanked back the covers and then gently pulled them over her. "This is definitely a fever. I'm going to call a doctor, and I'll get you some Tylenol."

She tossed restlessly under the covers. "I have a fever? I thought I just had a broken heart."

"Oh shit, baby." His voice was soft and broken. He leaned down to kiss her on the forehead. "Don't say things like that. I'll never forgive myself if I broke your heart."

"Well, you did." She didn't have the willpower to think through her words. They just spilled out. "Both of you did. You broke my heart."

10

_____

AFTER THAT CONVERSATION, THE DAY PASSED IN AN ACHING, heated blur.

Summer had no sense of how much time was passing. She knew she had a fever, and she knew she was in bed. And she knew that Lincoln was there a lot, wiping her face with a cool washcloth or making her drink. Sometimes she was glad he was there, reaching out to touch him or mumbling out his name. But sometimes he annoyed her, always hovering and dripping water on her when she was chilling.

It changed from moment to moment whether she needed him to help her or whether she wanted to just be left alone to suffer.

Mrs. Wilson came in at one point and tsked her tongue a lot. She set up soft, soothing music to play in the background and diffused some sort of essential oils that were cool and faintly minty. Neither thing troubled Summer unduly, and she knew the woman was trying to help, so she managed to force out thanks.

The doctor paid a house call. Doctors did that in Green

Valley. He wasn't much help. He told them she had the flu. He told her to get rest and drink a lot of fluids. He gave her a medication that was supposed to shorten the duration, but it didn't make her feel any better right now.

During the times when her fever was reduced, she remembered that Lincoln had broken up with her, which was almost worse than the fever.

That was how the day passed. Miserably. Interminably. And without much hope of getting better.

She fell asleep sometime in the middle of the afternoon. She had no idea how long she slept, but it was a relief to have any sort of break. She woke up as a brutal wave of heat slammed into her. She pushed down the covers desperately and half sat up, gasping out, "Lincoln!"

He didn't answer.

He'd always answered before. He'd always been right next to the bed. He'd wipe her hot face and murmur out soothing words.

She waited a minute, but he didn't appear. "Lincoln!" she choked out again. Her mouth was bone dry, and the rest of her body was drenched in sweat.

"I'm here!" The voice was slightly muffled. It took a minute to figure out it was coming from the connecting room. Then it was closer. Slightly breathless. "I'm here, baby."

She blinked in the direction of the voice and saw Lincoln approaching her bed. His hair was wet, and he was naked except for a towel wrapped around his waist.

He had a damp washcloth in his hand. He wiped her face and neck with it as she relaxed back onto the bed. It was cool.

Then he brought a bottle of water to her mouth so she could take a couple of swallows.

"Thank you." She blinked up at his handsome face.

His green eyes were so soft. "You're welcome. Sorry I wasn't here. You were asleep, so I thought I could take a quick shower."

"You're allowed to take a shower." She tossed restlessly, suddenly freezing. She fumbled urgently for the covers she'd pushed down just a minute ago.

Lincoln leaned over to help her pull them up to her shoulders.

"Why am I like this?" She tried to clear her vision so she could see his expression better.

"You're sick, baby." He brushed some damp strands of hair back from her face. His touch was so gentle. "You've got a really high fever. The doctor said it would go up and down, but it seems really high to me. I'm going to call him again if it gets any higher."

"I'm okay now. You can go put your clothes on if you want."

He made a soft huff. Maybe laughter. "I'll go in a minute."

His fingers were still stroking her cheek. She turned her face into his hand until he was palming it.

Even as sick as she was, she could read the expression on his face. More than affection. It was adoration. And she wanted so much to always see it there.

But she wouldn't always see it there. He'd broken things off. He wasn't going to let himself love her.

She started to shake.

"Oh please don't," he whispered, still holding her face.

"You love me." She wished her voice wasn't so pitiful, but it was all she could manage at the moment. "I know you love me."

He shook his head, his features twisting briefly. "I can't, baby. You know I can't."

"But—"

"I'll take care of you as long as you need me. I'll always be there when you need me. I promise you that. But I can't."

She was crying now without tears. Everything in her body and heart hurt. "But I need you... I need you to love me too."

"Oh shit, baby. Please don't do this." He got up and walked to the bathroom, returning a minute later with a freshly dampened washcloth. He wiped her face with it. Then he gave her a few more sips of water. Then he murmured, "I'm going to get dressed. I'll be right back."

She nodded mutely.

She knew the truth now.

It didn't matter how sweet and tender he was being, taking care of her while she was sick.

He wasn't going to change his mind.

THE NIGHT and the next day followed in the same state of heat, pain, and timelessness. All Summer wanted to do was sleep deeply, to stop aching, or at least to pass into unconsciousness for a while. But she wasn't given that grace.

In the evening of the second day, she managed to sleep for an hour or so. It was nice while it lasted, but it didn't last nearly long enough. She woke up as another wave of heat overwhelmed her, and she mumbled out what felt like her refrain. "Lincoln. Lincoln?"

"He's not here." The voice wasn't Lincoln's. She knew it,

NOELLE ADAMS

but she hadn't managed to open her eyes yet. She felt a damp cloth on her face. "But I'm here."

She opened her eyes to see a pair of kind brown eyes. "Carter."

He helped her take a few sips of water. "Yeah."

She really didn't want to sound ungrateful, so she managed to keep the whine out of her voice as she asked, "Did he need to get some sleep?"

"No. I don't think he's slept for two days. But he needed to go into work. He tried to take off, but they couldn't find a last-minute replacement, so he has to go in until they find someone to cover for him."

"Oh." She found the energy to smile at him. "Thanks for filling in. You really didn't have to."

"As if I wouldn't." He looked sad behind his smile. "You've always been there for me when I needed you. I'm not about to let you down."

Her eyes burned, but she was so parched she couldn't cry. "Thank you." She shifted uncomfortably, pushing down the hot covers. "Why aren't I getting any better?"

"The doctor said it would be a few days at least. Maybe a week."

"I thought that medicine was supposed to help."

"Sometimes it does—makes it shorter or not as bad."

"This seems pretty bad to me. I can't remember ever being this sick."

"I know." He stroked her face with the wet cloth. "I'm sorry you're going through it."

She sighed and tried to relax. Tried not to push his hand away just because she was feeling irritable. Carter was being so sweet. He'd always been so good-hearted.

And she'd hurt him. A lot. Maybe it wasn't her fault, but still... She'd done it.

"Do you think you could eat anything?"

She shook her head.

"Maybe try some Gatorade?"

She made a face. She didn't like the taste of that in the best of circumstances.

"Okay. Try to drink some more water then."

She tried, getting several swallows down until her stomach started churning. Then she flopped her head back onto the pillow and closed her eyes, completely exhausted.

"You want to watch TV or anything?"

"I can't focus on it. Thanks though."

She could tell Carter was trying to keep the conversation light. "Mom keeps coming in and putting on new music. She says it's *health music* and it's supposed to make you better quicker. I have no idea where she's getting it. I hope it's not annoying."

"It's fine. It's pretty neutral. It's nice of her to try to help. The essential oils are actually kind of nice."

"Oh good. I had to stop her from rubbing coconut oil all over you with more of those oils in them. I hope I did the right thing in not letting her."

She almost—almost—giggled. "Yes. You did the right thing. Thanks."

His expression relaxed. They smiled at each other for a minute.

Despite the pulsing ache of her body, it almost felt like they were friends again.

The brief conversation wore her out, so she tried to drift back to sleep. It was a long time before she did.

She woke up again with another surge of heat, mumbling out Lincoln's name.

When she didn't get a response, she was suddenly, irrationally terrified. She sat up straight in bed. "Lincoln! Lincoln!"

"Summer, I'm sorry. He's still not here." Carter's voice. The world was a heated blur, but she was conscious enough to identify it.

She felt a hand on her shoulder, trying to push her back down. She fought it instinctively. She had no idea what was happening. It felt like the whole world was assaulting her.

"Summer, please." Carter sounded almost desperate, and in any other situation, she would have immediately tried to help him. "Let me help you. I'm here."

"Lincoln," she choked out, trying to calm down, trying to make her mind work. A tiny part of her knew she shouldn't be struggling like this. It made no sense, and it was going to hurt Carter's feelings.

There was no logical reason why Carter couldn't take care of her just as well as Lincoln could. But she was far beyond logic at the moment.

Carter was still trying to get her to lie back on the bed. "Your fever has gone up. Maybe you're delirious or something. It's really okay. Let me help you."

She sobbed and couldn't stop. She kept struggling in Carter's hands. "Where's... *Lincoln*?"

"I'm here, baby." It was a new voice. From the doorway of the room. "I'm here now."

She sobbed some more—this time in relief.

Then Lincoln was kneeling beside the bed, gently easing her back down so her head was on the pillow. Carter handed him the washcloth, and Lincoln wiped her heated face with it. Wiped the tears away.

She couldn't focus enough to really see his face, but she didn't need to. She could *feel* him, and that was enough.

~

SHE EITHER FELL asleep or passed out eventually. Either way, she lost track of everything for a while.

The next thing she knew, her mind was clearer. She wasn't quite so oppressively hot. She managed to open her eyes just enough to peek through. It was mostly dark in the room. Neat and quiet except for the low accompaniment of Mrs. Wilson's *health music*. She turned her head and saw that Lincoln was in a chair next to the bed.

He was slouched down, his head lolling to the side. He was sound asleep.

Carter was no longer there, so he must have gone to bed. But Lincoln hadn't left. The poor thing must have been exhausted.

She wasn't going to wake him up even though her mouth was dry as a bone. She found the energy to reach over to the nightstand and take the bottle of water there. It was luke-warm, but she didn't care. She took several sips.

She needed to pee, but that could wait until Lincoln woke up.

She was fully focused on replacing the bottle of water without dropping it in her feeble grip, so she didn't realize Lincoln had moved until his hand was wrapping around her bottle to help her.

"I was doing it," she said. "You were sleeping."

"I wasn't sleeping." His voice was warm and soft and edged with dry amusement. "Just resting my eyes."

"Liar," she sniffed. "You should go to bed."

"I'm not going to go to bed until you can manage to wake up without screaming out my name."

"I was feverish! And I don't scream out your name."

He chuckled and caressed her face gently. "You definitely do scream out my name. I heard you all the way downstairs when I was coming back from work. You freaked poor Carter out." He paused a moment. "It feels like your fever has gone down."

"I think it has. I can think clearly again. Is Carter all right?"

"He's all right. Worried about you. He's got some important meetings tomorrow, so I told him to go bed."

"Good." She shifted uncomfortably. "Can you help me get to the bathroom? If not, there's going to be some unpleasant cleanup to take care of."

"Sure." He reached down to help her to her feet. "Mom brought up some clean sheets. If you want, I can change the bed while you're in there. You've sweated all over these."

"You don't have to make it sound so gross," she grumbled, leaning on him as she limped toward the bathroom.

"If you don't think it's gross, you can keep sleeping on sweaty sheets."

"No, I don't want to. Please change them. I just thought you might be nicer since I'm so sick and all."

He chuckled and nuzzled her hair before he evidently remembered he wasn't supposed to do that kind of thing. He jerked his head away and said, "Since when have I ever been nice?" They'd reached the bathroom now. "You need help in here?"

"No. I can manage. Close the door since I'm not too keen on you watching me pee. If you feel like changing the sheets, it would be appreciated."

She could hear him laughing behind the closed door of the bathroom, and she sat on the toilet with a smile on her face.

SHE FELT BETTER after she'd gone to the bathroom, washed her hands and face, and brushed her hair. She was feeling stronger, so she went back to the bedroom and got clean underwear and a nightgown to change into while Lincoln finished with the bed. She took some more Tylenol.

"I feel okay for now," she said after climbing under the deliciously cool sheets. "You should go get some rest."

"I'm fine."

"I'm serious. Carter said you haven't slept for two days, and you're going to pass out from exhaustion soon. I feel better right now. It feels like I might have a respite before the fever goes back up. So go lie on your bed at least. Leave the door open. If I scream out your name again, you'll hear me. But hopefully I won't."

He stood over her bed, his fingertips tracing the line of her cheekbone. "I don't mind if you do."

She smiled at him rather sappily. "Go lie down."

"Okay. I won't be sleeping, so just call out if you need anything. The door will be open. I'll hear you."

She felt better when he went to his room, leaving the connecting door wide open.

She felt so good she fell asleep.

THE NEXT TIME she woke up, someone was coming into the room. It was dark, and she'd slept deeply, and for once she hadn't woken up in a hot haze of fever. She felt a presence beside her bed, but she couldn't focus enough to identify it or open her eyes.

After a minute, she felt it move away without doing or saying anything. This provoked her curiosity enough to open her eyes just a little.

She saw Carter at the door that connected her room to Lincoln's. His back was to her, but he was dressed in a business suit. It must be morning, and he was heading into work.

"Hey." The voice was Lincoln's and faintly groggy, like he'd just woken up.

"Sorry to wake you," Carter said. He was talking softly, like he didn't want to disturb Summer. Then, as she watched, he stepped into Lincoln's room. "Just checking on her."

"She was a little better earlier. Her fever had gone down. Is she still sleeping?" Lincoln's voice was more awake now, and it was moving closer. He'd probably gotten out of bed, although she couldn't see either of the men at the moment.

"Yes. She's sleeping."

"Okay." Lincoln's tone was different now. Almost wary for some reason. "Is something going on?"

"I wanted to say something."

Summer's breath hitched. Her body grew perfectly still.

She suddenly knew what was coming, and she loved Carter so much for it.

Lincoln said, "What is it? I've had a hard few days, so I'm not really up for heart-to-hearts at the moment."

"Yeah. I know. But I'm going to say this anyway. Just once. You can do with it whatever you want."

"Okay." Lincoln's one word was drawn out very slowly.

"I forgive you."

The simple words lingered in the air. Summer was starting to shake under the covers.

Lincoln didn't answer for a long stretch of time. Then finally he asked in a hoarse whisper, "What?"

"I forgive you. That's it."

"That can't be it. I—"

"You messed up. A lot. I know you did. And some of the things you messed up hurt me."

"I more than hurt you. I destroyed your relationship with Dad. He never trusted you after I let you down. It's my fault you were stuck in the position you were in when he died. My fault you were so desperate. You know it as well as I did."

"Yeah. I know. But most of that was Dad's fault. He was never going to change. I blamed you because it hurt too much to admit the truth about Dad to myself. But it's been years now. I shouldn't still be holding on to it."

"You have every right to hold on to it. I didn't do it to screw you over. I was... scared. Scared to be real. Scared to take life seriously. I was afraid it would hurt me again, the way it hurt when Dad rejected me. But that's no excuse for what I did to you. Then and so many other times before. I always let you down when you needed me." Lincoln's voice was almost broken. Summer couldn't see his face, but she could well imagine it. Tears ached in her eyes and slowly streamed down her cheeks.

"Not always. You didn't let me down this year." Carter's voice cracked just slightly. He was always more controlled than his brother. "You did everything I needed you to do, even though you believed it was wrong. Summer said she loves the man you are now. That she trusts the man you are now. And it made me... it made me realize I should do the same thing."

"You shouldn't do anything of the kind." Lincoln was speaking in no more than a rasp now. "You should hate me. Forever. I'm the sinner, remember? I don't deserve your forgiveness."

"Maybe not." There was a slight pause. "But you're getting it anyway."

"Carter—"

"Stop arguing. You've messed up. You've hurt people you didn't want to hurt. Just like all the rest of us. Just like I messed up only a few weeks ago. You didn't hold that against me. You came to get me. So I'm coming to get you right now. You've made mistakes. It doesn't mean you can't be loved. I love you. Summer loves you." For the first time, his voice broke for real.

"You can't—"

"I can do anything I want to do. I love Summer, and I want her to be happy. And I want the same thing for you. She loves you. You're the one who makes her happy, who lets her be the person she really wants to be. I was holding on to my resentment, so I didn't want to see it before. But I see it now. So if you love me, if you want to do something to make up for the past, then love her. *Love* her. And don't ever let her down."

"But... wait!" Lincoln sounded almost desperate.

Carter was suddenly in the doorway between the rooms. He didn't look over at her bed as he strode to the door and disappeared into the hallway.

Lincoln tried to follow him but stopped when Carter closed the door behind him. Then he stood in the middle of Summer's bedroom, facing the door his brother had just shut. He ducked his head. His shoulders shook slightly.

Summer made a whimpering sound and rolled out of bed, stumbling over toward him.

He didn't turn toward her, so she wrapped her arms around him from behind.

He shook even more. He felt broken in her arms. It took a couple of minutes before he pulled himself together.

"I'm okay," he mumbled, turning around. "I'm okay. You shouldn't be out of bed. You shouldn't have heard that."

"Then you shouldn't have had the conversation with the door open." She hugged him from the front, relieved when he wrapped his arms around her for a few seconds. "He's a really great brother."

"Yeah." Lincoln cleared his throat and straightened up, rubbing his face with both hands. "Yeah, he is. How are you feeling?"

"I'm okay. Weak and pitiful and achy, but not so feverish."

"Well, let's get you back to bed." He turned her around, one arm around her.

She fought the grip. "Actually, I need to go to the bathroom and then I might take a shower, if you don't mind helping."

"Of course I'll help."

They went into the bathroom together. While Lincoln

turned on the water, Summer stripped off her panties and gown.

Lincoln blinked in surprise when he turned around to find her naked. She saw his eyes run up and down her body greedily before he jerked his gaze away.

Ridiculously, she almost giggled at how hard he was trying not to leer at her.

"You can get in the shower too," she said, stepping over and putting a hand over his heart.

"Summer—"

"I might need help in there. I'm still really weak."

"You're sick. You're not thinking clearly. I can't—"

"You can get into the shower with me, Lincoln. Nothing is going to happen. I guarantee I don't feel up to sex right now. But I need you. I *need* you."

That seemed to reach him. He nodded and helped her into the large, tiled shower. Then he shucked his clothes and got in too.

She let the warm water spray over her, streaming down her hair and skin. Then she pulled Lincoln into a tight hug.

He wrapped his arms around her. He held her as the water cascaded around both of them. She shook with emotion and relief and weakness and hope.

Hope.

He was holding her so tightly. She could feel the emotion wrack him.

Something had changed. She knew it. He wasn't holding back like he had before.

He needed her just as much as she needed him, and she wasn't going to let his stubbornness get in the way of what they could have.

Carter had done it. He'd changed things. He was the best friend she'd ever had in the world.

But Lincoln was the man she loved, and she was going to love him forever.

SUMMER WAS sick for three more days. Her fever never got as bad as it had on the first two days, and she was finally able to keep a little food down, but her temperature kept going up and down every hour or two, paired with a sore throat, headache, and body aches.

It felt like she'd been sick forever. Like she was missing out on life. Including very important things like finalizing the Wilson Hotels acquisition.

On the day the final contract was signed, Summer felt well enough to go downstairs. She didn't have the energy to get dressed and leave the house. The illness had completely wiped her out. But she took a shower. Put on a clean T-shirt and yoga pants. And went downstairs at about five thirty.

She had enough energy to chat for a little while with Mrs. Wilson before the older woman left to have dinner with some friends. Then, hungrier than she'd been in days, Summer puttered in the kitchen, looking for something she felt like eating.

Carter found her there, leaning over to look in a drawer of the refrigerator.

"You're up."

She straightened up and whirled around, smiling at the sound of his voice. "Finally."

"Are you feeling better?"

"I am. Not great still, but way better. Thanks for all your help."

He shrugged. "It was no problem." He was dressed in one of his regular business suits, and he looked handsome and professional. And also utterly exhausted. His tie was slightly loosened, and he took off his suit coat while she watched. "You looking for something to eat? There's some homemade soup in there."

"I know. But all I've had all week is soup. I'm looking for something a little more substantial."

"Ah." He gave her a familiar smile and came over to stand in front of the refrigerator beside her. "Somewhere in here there's half a leftover chicken potpie that Mom brought home yesterday. All we'd have to do is warm it up."

Summer perked up. "That sounds perfect. It hasn't been eaten, has it?"

"It's got to be here. No one's been around who would have eaten it." He dug out a covered container from behind some fresh produce. "Here it is."

"Yum. Will you eat with me?"

"Yeah. I'm hungry too."

They heated the potpie up and poured ginger ale over ice in their glasses. Then they sat at the kitchen table to eat.

Summer was almost happy as she took her first bite. Then she reached over to put a hand on Carter's arm. "How did things go today? No problems?"

"No problems. Lincoln came through. It's all done."

"I'm so glad." She hesitated before she added, "I guess he has to work this evening."

"Yeah. He went over early to the bar to do something.

Open up for a delivery or something. But everything's good. It's all over."

She nodded as she took another bite. That meant the reason for her marriage to Lincoln had also ended. They could get divorced now with no harm to the acquisition.

She hoped he didn't want to, but he hadn't said anything yet.

"Have you decided on your plans to redo the new properties?" she asked.

"Yeah. I think so. We're going to split the difference between my timeline and Lincoln's."

Her eyes widened. "Really."

Carter's expression wasn't guarded. He looked natural. Slightly sheepish. "Yeah. I don't think we need to move as slow as he wanted to move, but he was right about being a little more careful. I didn't want to hear it from him because... well, because I didn't want to hear anything from him. But he wasn't wrong. I don't want to blow through your investment and have it come to nothing. I want this whole thing to be worth it to you."

She'd been eating, since the potpie was good, but at that she put down her fork and reached over to cover Carter's hand on the table. "It's worth it. It's already worth it to me, even if Lincoln never... It's worth it."

"Thank you. But I want to make money for you, if we can. Or at least give the money you gave us back. So I'm not going to rush. Part of me still feels kind of... desperate." He looked down at his half-eaten plate of food. "Wanting to prove stuff to Dad even though he's dead."

"I know."

He finally met her eyes. "But I'm trying to work through

that and make good business decisions. I think we've got a good plan. I think we can save the brand and the company. We're going to try our best."

"Lincoln's still planning to give you the company, isn't he?"

"Yeah. He said he'd still like to be involved, if I'll let him—which of course I will—but he knows he's not equipped to run the whole thing. Honestly, I'm not sure I'm equipped either."

"You are. I know you are, Carter. You're going to do great."

"I hope so. I'll try my best." He let out a long breath and then smiled at her. "I've missed you."

Her smile in response was a little wobbly. "I've missed you too. I'm so glad to have you back."

"I was afraid for a while that I'd lost you."

"Well, you didn't. You're not going to. You're keeping me, and you're also getting your brother back. So hopefully that's... that's..."

"I'm not sure I'd ever have gotten my brother back without you," he said quietly, soberly. "So thank you for that. Has..." Carter cleared his throat. "Has Lincoln said anything to you yet?"

She shook her head. "Not yet. But I think... I think he will. What you said to him made a real difference. I know how hard that must have been for you to do. I can never thank you enough."

"You don't have to. I should have done it ages ago. The situation I'm in is entirely my fault—for being blind about you for so long. It's not Lincoln's fault. And it's definitely not your fault."

He was trying to be casual, but his features looked too

tight. Just slightly pained. It made Summer's heart twist. "Are you okay, Carter?"

"I don't know. But I'm making it. And I'll be okay eventually."

A single tear streamed out of her eye as she reached over to squeeze his hand again. "You'll be better than okay. You're going to find someone who blows the roof off your world in a way I've never done. And she's going to love you more than anything because everything about you deserves to be loved. You're going to be so happy, Carter. I know you will."

His mouth twisted briefly into almost a smile. "Maybe," he rasped.

"No maybe. I know it for sure. Because if anyone should be loved like that, it's you."

THAT EVENING, Summer was determined to talk to Lincoln. If he'd changed his mind about their relationship, she wanted to know right now. And if he wasn't going to change his mind, then she needed to know that too.

So she took a long bath and rubbed on scented lotion and dressed in the pretty black chemise that Lincoln had teased her about on the day she moved in. Then she climbed into Lincoln's bed, found a show to watch on television, and she tried to stay awake until Lincoln returned from work.

She really tried.

Didn't succeed, however.

She made it until midnight—she knew because she looked at the clock and mentally patted herself on the back for staying awake so long—but sometime after that she drifted off. The next thing she knew was Lincoln climbing into the bed beside her.

"Lincoln," she mumbled as she became aware of his scent surrounding her and the feel of the mattress shifting with his weight. "You're finally here."

"What are you doing here, baby?" He didn't sound annoyed or particularly surprised. He sounded slightly amused and very tender.

"Waiting for you. I tried to stay awake." She scooted over until she was pressed against his side. He was wearing his pajama pants, and he smelled like he'd just taken a shower.

He chuckled as he wrapped an arm around her. "Well, you didn't do a very good job."

"Well, it's late, and I was tired."

"I know you are." He pressed a few kisses against her hair. "You've been sick. You should be sleeping in your own bed and getting better."

"I'm better. Just tired. And it took you forever to get here."

The pause that followed was a little longer than it should have been. "I know it did. I know it did. But I'm here now."

The rasp in his voice went straight to her heart. She blinked to clear her vision and lifted her head so she could see his face.

The television was still running, and it lit his face enough for her to see his expression. He was gazing at her with his heart in his eyes.

She made a silly little whimper as hope leaped from her chest to her throat. "Lincoln?"

"I love you, baby. I love you so much."

"Yeah?"

"Yeah." He lifted a hand to stroke her hair back from her

face very gently, as if she might break. "You knew that already, didn't you?"

"Yeah. Yeah, I knew."

"Didn't do a good job hiding my feelings, did I?"

"No. You're not very good at that."

"I know I'm not. I'm surprised it wasn't painfully obvious the day of the funeral how completely gone I am on you. Did you know it then?"

"No. I didn't. I thought you were just being mean. But I put a few things together afterward. You were too... you were too angry about my feelings for Carter."

"I feel like maybe I've loved you forever. Like I've been waiting all this time, watching you, wanting to see you..."

When he hesitated, Summer slanted him a teasing look. "If you dare to say something maudlin like *bloom*..."

He laughed out loud and pulled her into a soft hug until she was cuddled halfway on top of him. "Not bloom. But maybe... come alive. Show the rest of the world who you've always been, who I've always known you to be. I feel like I've always been watching and wanting you, even when I was too clueless to know what these feelings meant."

She kissed his chest since it was the closest part of his body to her lips. "Maybe I was waiting for you," she whispered, too emotional to speak in her normal voice.

His arms tightened. "Maybe so. I know I don't deserve you. And part of me is still terrified that one day you'll wake up and... come to your senses... decide the feelings for Carter have come back now that he wants you in the same way."

"Lincoln, stop it!" She straightened enough to give him a sharp glare. "I don't ever want to hear anything like that again. I love Carter. I always will. I'm in love with you."

He pulled her face toward him so he could kiss her lips softly. "I guess I'm still a sinner because I'm not noble enough to keep saying no, when you're everything I've always wanted."

She kissed him back before she dissolved into blissful giggles. "Good. That's exactly how it should be. You need to stay a sinner all your life if it means you'll let me love you, because I'm never going to stop."

"Me either," he murmured thickly, rolling her onto her back and moving over so he could kiss her more fully. "This is it for me. You get that, right?"

"Yeah. I get it."

"So..." He pulled out of the kiss so he could meet her gaze. "So what do you think about not getting divorced like we planned? Do you think you might want to stay married to me for a while?"

She tried to smile and respond in a clear, articulate way, but her response was another helpless giggle.

He arched his eyebrows. "Was that a yes?"

"Yes, that was a yes. You need to get better at interpreting the sounds I make, even when they don't form traditional words."

"Is that right?"

"Yes, that's right. Sometimes I'm communicating without words, and you need to understand what I'm telling you."

His hands started moving under her chemise, stroking her belly and sliding up to her breasts. She made a little yelp of surprise when he tweaked her nipple.

His voice was deliciously teasing as he mouthed her neck and murmured, "So just so I get some practice. That little sound meant *Oh fuck, Lincoln, you make me feel good. Please, please do it again. I'm begging you.* Didn't it?"

Her body was definitely starting to respond to his touches, but she couldn't give in too easily. So she sniffed and said coolly, "Something like that, but without the unnecessary stroking of your ego."

His chuckle wafted against the sensitive skin at the crook of her neck. He gave her a little nip that made her arch and gasp and then fondled both her breasts until she was moaning helplessly. "And that particular sound means *No one in the world touches me like you do. No one makes me feel as good as you do. Never, ever stop.* Am I right?"

"Well..." She was shifting restlessly as arousal tightened inside her. He was still kissing and caressing her even as he teased her. "That was quite a bit more inflated than I'd ever say out loud, but you're not wrong in theory. Better keep practicing."

He pulled her chemise off over her head and gazed down hotly at her naked body. "Oh fuck, baby. I love you so much. But I'll never deserve you."

She reached up and took his face in both her hands. "It doesn't matter. That's not what this is about. I love you too. I love you, Lincoln. That's what this is about."

He kissed her deeply and kept kissing her as his hands moved over her body. It wasn't long before she was wet and urgent with desire, and he was tense above her. She squeezed her hands down until she could reach his erection. She stroked him through the fabric of his pants until he broke the kiss and groaned.

Both of them were suddenly desperate, as if the last threads of their control had snapped. They fumbled to get his pants off and then fumbled to get in position, and then both of them cried out when he pushed into her and she wrapped her legs around his waist.

He kept trying to kiss her as he started to rock. When their motion became too fast and hard, his face was still only inches from hers. He grunted as he worked up toward climax, and she was gasping and whimpering as her own pleasure tightened too.

She came—hard and helpless and messy as she sobbed with emotion as much as the sensations. Then he was coming too, muttering out how much he loved her, how he would always love her, how she was the only one he ever wanted.

They lay together in a hot, sated tangle afterward. Even if Summer had had the energy to move, she wouldn't have wanted to.

She wanted to stay like this. Lincoln between her arms and legs. Loving her and letting her love him. Giving to her and taking what she was giving him. Pouring himself into her and allowing her to do the same.

He was her husband, and he was going to stay that way.

She got to hold on to him—exactly like this—for the rest of her life.

TWO MONTHS LATER, Summer got out of a quick shower and threw on a little pink robe before she ran out to the kitchen to check the lasagna in the oven.

It still had twenty minutes to go, based on the cooking time on the recipe, but she wasn't going to take any chances.

She and Lincoln were having their first dinner party this evening, and she wasn't going to mess up the main course.

They'd moved from the Wilson mansion into the large condo she owned—in one of the two luxury buildings right on the lakeside. It still felt new and exciting to live only with Lincoln even though they'd moved more than a month ago now. She got a silly little thrill when she left the kitchen and saw Lincoln sitting at the desk in the office nook, staring at a computer with his head propped on one hand.

"How's it going?" she asked as she passed.

"Terrible. What the hell was I thinking?"

"You were thinking it might be nice to get a college degree, so you're taking one class to try it out. If you decide you don't want to do it, you don't have to. But don't give up on the second week of class."

He made a face at her, but she knew he was playing it up on purpose. He'd been hesitant about making the decision since he still sometimes felt like his mistakes in the past had bound him to only one life. But he'd also been excited when he registered for an online introduction to business course at a nearby university.

She knew, deep down, he wanted to do this even though he'd never really let himself admit it, so she was going to make sure he didn't give up. She came over to peer at the computer screen, putting her hand on his shoulder as she leaned to look. "What's so terrible about it? It's not hard already, is it?"

"No, it's not hard. It's boring. Stupid. Any idiot would know this stuff."

She laughed and ran her hand through his hair, tweaking his ear as she withdrew. "In my experience, you have to get through a lot of boring, stupid stuff in college to get to the helpful stuff."

He groaned but then pushed back the desk chair and pulled her down into his lap. "I can think of better things to be doing right now than boring, stupid stuff."

"Well, if you're thinking about sex stuff, you can think again. People are going to start showing up in fifteen minutes."

They'd invited a few of Summer's friends and a few of Lincoln's. Plus Carter, of course.

Things had been going well with Carter for the past two months. He and Summer were back to being friends the way they used to. He never said anything about any other feelings. She didn't know if they'd gone away or if he was working through them in private. Either way, he was making sure not to make her feel sad or guilty about them, which was a very kind, Carter-like instinct.

He and Lincoln had been spending more time together too. Carter had taken over the company now officially, but he was allowing Lincoln to stay involved. Summer knew that meant a lot to Lincoln. If he decided to complete his college degree, Summer was pretty sure there would be a job waiting for him with the company. That was still in the future, but it was a possibility.

If he decided he'd rather stay a bartender, then that would be just fine too.

She wanted him to be happy—whatever that looked like. Happy in a way he'd never let himself be before.

He looked happy right now with his arms around her and that hot, soft, laughing look in his green eyes. "Fifteen minutes will be more than enough time for what I have in mind."

"You don't get fifteen minutes!" She struggled playfully in his grip. "You only get ten. I need at least five minutes to clean up the sperminess and throw on some clothes, unless you want me to greet our guests in this bathrobe."

"No way in hell you're doing that. Only I get to see you like this." He kissed her hard and quick. Then set her on her feet, stood up, and threw her over his shoulder. "Okay. Ten minutes it is."

She squealed in surprise and laughter as she hung over his shoulder, both off-balanced and exhilarated. "You only have nine minutes now, so you better move quick. None of your normal teasing and torture."

He was laughing too as he dropped her onto their bed. "Are you actually complaining that I take my time with you? You seem to be pretty happy with the kind of teasing and torture I provide."

She reached up to drag him down on top of her by fistfuls of his T-shirt. "I'm more than pretty happy. I'm as happy as a girl can get."

He met her eyes, and her heart melted at the expression she could see there. Love. Trust. Desire. Naked adoration. "I'll spend my life keeping you happy," he murmured thickly. "I promise you that, baby."

"I promise the same thing to you." She cupped his face tenderly for a long moment. But then she glanced over the clock. "Okay. You just used up two of your minutes on sappiness."

He laughed and opened her robe, lowering his mouth to one

of her breasts. But he slanted her a sly little look with a twitch of his eyebrows before he added, "But you're going to get a minute or two of torture for that reference to sperminess. You know how I feel about that. But I'll still get us done on time. I promise."

Lincoln kept that promise. As well as every other promise he made.

EPILOGUE

Six months later, Summer was sitting on a stool at Lincoln's bar, studiously peering at her phone and trying her best not to glance over to see what he was doing.

They were in a fight.

A really stupid fight.

But he was the one in the wrong, so she wasn't going to be the one to initiate a reconciliation. The most she would do was make herself available for an apology by coming into the bar this evening instead of staying at home and moping about all of Lincoln's bad qualities.

So here she was, pretending to scan through Twitter on her phone and sipping her drink.

When she'd come in and sat down, she'd felt like one of her normal daiquiris, but Lincoln had mixed one for her without even asking first, which she thought was obnoxiously presumptuous, so she'd given him a cool sniff and said she actually wanted a whiskey sour.

She didn't particularly like whiskey sours. She'd just said the first thing that came to her that Lincoln would never have guessed. He was far too arrogant and needed to be taken down a few pegs.

He'd just arched his annoying eyebrows and gone to make her the drink, presenting it to her with a flourish when he was done.

So now she was trying to get down the whole whiskey sour so he wouldn't think he'd scored a point against her.

The asshole still hadn't apologized, and she wasn't going to let him win.

She was still focusing with laser-like precision on her phone, struggling not to observe Lincoln's friendly conversation with the regulars sitting at the bar and the others who came up to order more drinks.

He was acting like nothing was wrong, but she knew he was doing it on purpose. He wasn't all that hard to read, and she could see tension in his shoulders and that he occasionally slanted her looks when he thought she wouldn't notice.

He wanted the fight to be over too.

But he knew what he had to do to make that happen.

She wasn't going to do it for him.

She loved the obnoxious asshole, but she was in the right here. He needed to apologize first.

She was growing impatient with staring at her phone, however. As soon as she forced down the rest of her drink, she would go over and chat with Lance Carlyle and Savannah Emerson, who'd come into the bar a few minutes ago and were sitting at a table with some friends. They were always entertaining, and they'd distract her from Lincoln.

She was peering at her phone so determinedly that she didn't even notice when Savannah approached. Not until the other woman sat down beside her.

"Are we in an argument with Lincoln tonight?" Savannah asked in a hushed tone of exaggerated subterfuge.

Summer giggled. "Yes. We are."

"What did he do to us this time?" Savannah had big blue-gray eyes and a pretty, clever, and expressive face. She was giving Summer a sly smile.

"He was an asshole. Unsurprisingly." Summer considered Savannah a good friend now, but she wasn't going to give the details of the argument. Even a stupid, trivial argument like the one she'd had with Lincoln this morning was part of their intimate relationship. It was private. She wasn't going to spill to the world.

"So you're sitting here waiting for him to step down off his high horse and make it better?"

"Yes. Exactly. He's being very slow about stepping. The man is ridiculously stubborn." Summer risked a quick look over and saw Lincoln pouring three glasses of white wine for a group of young women. He glanced over and met her eyes with a dry, fond amusement that went right to her heart. But she was strong. She narrowed her eyes coldly and turned back toward her friend.

Savannah was laughing openly. "You two are hilarious."

"For someone who argues with her husband as much as you do, I'm not sure you've got any grounds for comment."

"Lance and I enjoy arguing most of the time. I'm not sure you really do. You should do something to speed things up."

"I would," Summer admitted. "That's why I came here. But I can't think of anything else to do now that I'm here."

"I'm good at this sort of thing. I'll think of something." Savannah propped her head on her hand and thought for a minute. "I've got it. I'll get Lance over here to flirt with you.

That will get Lincoln going for sure. He's pretty possessive, isn't he? He always gets annoyed when guys flirt with you. I'd see him bristling about it long before you and he got together."

"Really?" Summer couldn't help but like this piece of information.

"Of course really. He was into you for a long time. Didn't you know that? I'd see all kinds of soulful looks aimed in your direction over the years whenever you came to the bar." Savannah straightened up and pulled out her phone from her purse. "So what do you say? You want to try it? I'll text Lance right now and tell him to get on the job."

Summer shook her head reluctantly. "It's a good idea, but it won't work. He likes Lance. They're friends. He'd know Lance would never flirt with me."

"That's true. Oh, I know." Savannah started texting quickly. "I'll tell Lance to put Chris up to it. Chris is a friend of his visiting from grad school, so Lincoln has no idea who he is. I bet Chris will do it."

Summer was torn between giggling embarrassment and excitement. She never would have thought of such a thing herself, but the plan was too tempting to refuse. Plus Savannah had already finished whatever message she'd texted to her husband.

Savannah's eyes sparkled. "This is going to be so good. I'll head back. Chris should be over here in just a minute. Don't blow it by getting too nervous or embarrassed."

"I'll do my best, but I'm not as good at this sort of thing as you are."

"You'll do just fine. Just think about how obnoxious Lincoln is sometimes."

Summer took her friend's advice and reviewed a long list of Lincoln's obnoxiousness as Savannah left the bar to return to her husband and friends.

Summer wasn't good at a lot of things, and one of them was holding on to resentment. All through her mental list of grievances, other things kept popping into her mind. All the things she loved about Lincoln—from his laughing green eyes to all the lengths he went to in order to make her happy.

So she wasn't exactly stewing when an attractive man who looked around thirty sauntered over and took the stool Savannah had vacated. Chris leaned over toward her and murmured, "I was volunteered for this mission. I'm supposed to act like I'm coming on to you."

Summer giggled stupidly. "Sorry you got dragged into it. You're clearly a very good friend."

"Hey, you're not exactly unpleasant to be close to. I might come on to you for real if you weren't already taken." Chris reached over and lightly stroked her forearm, which was resting on the bar. He leaned even closer, smiling in a flirtatious way.

Summer blushed dark red and forced herself not to look over at Lincoln. She smiled at Chris. Laughed. Didn't pull her arm away from him even though she didn't want another man touching her, even so casually.

She held out as long as she could. When her eyes finally wrenched over in Lincoln's direction, she immediately saw that the plan had worked.

Lincoln was scowling fiercely and striding over in their direction. Before Summer knew what was happening, he'd come around the bar, taken Chris by the back collar of his shirt, and hauled him off the stool by force.

Chris was a good sport. He was grinning as he returned to Lance and Savannah, who were both laughing their heads off.

Summer was giggling helplessly when Lincoln took the stool he'd cleared of Chris. He gave her a narrow look. "I can't believe you recruited other people into this thing."

"Hey, I didn't do a thing. Savannah had an idea. She's smart like that."

Lincoln's expression softened deliciously. He cupped her face in one hand. "And you know perfectly well that I wouldn't let some other guy get handsy with my wife."

"He wasn't really handsy. He was just—"

He leaned over to kiss her. "I'm sorry, baby. The whole thing was my fault. I was a dick. And I know better than to treat you that way."

"Good. I'm glad to hear it." She pulled away from him to realize that half the bar was watching them, most of them grinning. Savannah and Lance's table was applauding.

Lincoln gave her one more quick kiss before he stood up. "I'll apologize more later when my shift is over. You going home?"

"I might go hang out with Savannah and them for a while. I'll see how much energy I have."

He stroked her loose hair before he reluctantly stepped away.

Summer went to hang out, assuming she'd only stay a little while before heading back to their condo. But she had a great time, so she ended up staying a couple of hours.

About half an hour after she'd joined Savannah's table, Carter came into the bar with a date. Summer couldn't remember the young woman's name. This was just a first or second date. She was pretty and smiling, but Summer could tell from Carter's expression that this probably wasn't going to turn into something serious.

Carter waved at Summer when he saw her, and she watched as he and his date walked up to the bar. She saw him extend a hand toward Lincoln, and she smiled when Lincoln reached over the bar to take it.

The two men didn't talk for very long, but the gesture made her happy. They'd been getting along well for the past several months. They were closer now than she'd ever known them to be.

It was important to her. It meant a lot. For both their sakes.

Savannah must have seen her watching the Wilson brothers, because the other woman murmured, "I haven't seen Carter with Tiff before. Is it serious?"

"No. I don't think so."

"He hasn't dated anyone serious for a long time."

"Yeah. No, he hasn't." Summer sighed. Carter seemed happy enough. She was pretty sure he'd gotten over whatever he'd been feeling for her early in the year. But she wanted him to be even happier.

"He needs to find a girl. If anyone deserves to find the love of his life, it's Carter." It was like Savannah had read her mind.

"I'd love it if he did, but no sign of it yet."

"Maybe we can help. Would he let us set him up, do you think?"

"I... don't know. Maybe."

"I think we should. I think we should call on every resource and make it our mission to find the right girl for him. I bet we could get him married off by the end of the year if we really work at it."

Summer glanced over at her friend. "Are you serious?"

"Yeah. Why not? He's obviously not having any success finding her on his own. Maybe he just needs our help. You want to?"

With a shrug, Summer said, "Yeah. I guess it's worth a try. Let's work on it."

～

SUMMER TOOK a bath when she got back home. It was a Friday evening, so she was in no particular hurry to get to bed. She wanted to be awake when Lincoln returned so they could talk. So they could really make up.

She was dressed in pretty pink lingerie—a silk chemise and matching robe—and finishing a glass of wine on the couch when Lincoln got back.

"Still awake?" he asked, dropping his keys on the entry table and strolling over to where she was stretched out on the couch. "You're usually asleep on Friday evenings."

"I guess I had extra energy tonight." She smiled at him, pleased when he lowered himself to the sofa, rearranging her slightly so he could climb on top of her.

"Energy for what?" he murmured.

"For you." She wrapped her arms around him.

He kissed her slow and sweet for a minute. Then he raised his head and met her eyes. "Hey, I am sorry about this morning."

"I know you are. You were sorry as soon as it happened."

"I know none of it was your fault. I shouldn't have blamed you."

Lincoln had been scheduled to attend a Wilson Hotels meeting that morning, and he'd overslept since he'd worked late at the bar. Summer had tried to wake him up when she'd gotten out of the shower and seen he wasn't yet up. He'd muttered, "Yeah, I'm awake," when she'd poked him, so she'd gone to work on drying her hair, which was always a long process.

When she returned to the bedroom, she'd seen he was still sleeping, so she'd tried again. When he was finally awake, he was rushed and urgent since he was anxious about being late for the meeting when Carter was counting on him. He'd snapped at her repeatedly, blaming her for not getting him up on time. That had led to the bad-tempered argument they'd started the day with.

"I really thought you were awake the first time," she said, stroking his thick hair and playing with his earlobe. "I never would have let you oversleep on purpose."

"I know that. But it wouldn't have been your fault even then. I'm an adult. I'm responsible for getting up on time for meetings." He nuzzled her neck before he added, "I was so grumpy because I'm so scared of letting Carter down."

"I know that, Lincoln. I know why you were so panicked about it. Were you late?"

"Just a few minutes. It was no problem."

"And the meeting went well?"

"Yeah. It was good. Everything's going good. And the truth is I'm starting to think that it might have been okay even if I had been later." He cleared his throat. "Maybe... maybe things are going good enough between us that it won't all fall apart from one little thing."

She tightened her arms, hugging him close. "I think that's right. I'm so glad they're going good."

Lincoln was still working on getting his degree online. He was taking more classes now and had a schedule laid out to finish in a year and a half. He was only involved in Wilson Hotels unofficially, but so far the arrangement was working for all of them.

Summer had hope for the future. And—what was even more meaningful—Lincoln did too.

They hugged for a couple of minutes, wrapped up in each other both emotionally and physically. Then Lincoln started to shift. His body started to tighten.

Summer knew he was ready for more.

So was she.

Because she thought she knew what was going to happen, she was surprised when Lincoln gave a soft groan and pushed himself up off the couch. "Where are you going?" she asked, blinking and confused.

"Hold on," he murmured, striding into the bedroom and then returning in just a few seconds with something behind his back.

"What's that?" she asked, moving into a sitting position since Lincoln's expression was different now. Somewhere between nervous and excitement.

"I have something for you," he said, bringing his hand around to the front to show her a jeweler's box.

"You didn't have to get me anything!" She was smiling though. She liked presents, and Lincoln's presents were always particularly fun and meaningful.

"I wanted to." His expression twisted slightly. He really was anxious about this.

"Well," she demanded, her heart starting to race although she wasn't even sure why. "Are you going to give it to me?"

"Yes. I am. Now." He was gripping the box. His body gave a weird, rocking motion as if he were having to force himself to do the next thing.

Then he did it.

His strong, lean body lowered onto one knee.

Summer gaped at him.

His handsome face twisted again—this time with wry self-consciousness. "I can't believe I'm doing this."

"What *are* you doing?" she gasped, moving toward the edge of the soft seat.

"I'm giving you this." He opened the box and extended it toward her. "With all the clichéd, sentimental trappings. Because you deserve it. You deserve everything. And I want to give it to you."

In the box was a pretty emerald-cut diamond on a gold band.

She was consumed by a surge of shocked joy and absolute love. But it was so strong that she couldn't move for a moment.

"I know we have the wedding rings. And that they're enough." He was searching her face, obviously trying to read her response. "But I wanted you to have this too. I know it's backward. But I'm always kind of backward. And just because you're stuck with me doesn't mean you should be left out of anything you might—"

She tackled him. Literally. She knocked both of them to

the floor with the force of her enthusiasm. "Yes! Yes, I want it! Thank you so much!"

Fortunately, he kept a grip on the ring so he was able to untangle them, find her hand, and slip the ring on her finger.

"There," he said, grinning nakedly, no hint of irony in his eyes. "Now we're engaged to be married for the rest of our lives."

"Thank you, thank you, thank you." She admired the ring rather sappily. "You didn't just get this today, did you?"

"No. I got it a couple of weeks ago. I was waiting for the right time to give it to you."

"And tonight was finally the right time?"

He kissed her. "Tonight was finally the right time."

ABOUT NOELLE ADAMS

Noelle handwrote her first romance novel in a spiral-bound notebook when she was twelve, and she hasn't stopped writing since. She has lived in eight different states and currently resides in Virginia, where she writes full time, reads any book she can get her hands on, and offers tribute to a very spoiled cocker spaniel.

She loves travel, art, history, and ice cream. After spending far too many years of her life in graduate school, she has decided to reorient her priorities and focus on writing contemporary romances. For more information, please check out her website: noelle-adams.com.

Made in the USA
Columbia, SC
05 September 2023

22521423R00150